Leslie Keith

The Mischief-Maker

Vol. 2

Leslie Keith

The Mischief-Maker
Vol. 2

ISBN/EAN: 9783337424435

Printed in Europe, USA, Canada, Australia, Japan

Cover: Foto ©Andreas Hilbeck / pixelio.de

More available books at **www.hansebooks.com**

THE MISCHIEF-MAKER.

THE MISCHIEF-MAKER.

BY

LESLIE KEITH,

Author of
" The Indian Uncle," " 'Lisbeth," " The Chilcotes," etc.

In Two Volumes.

Vol. II.

LONDON:

RICHARD BENTLEY & SON,

PUBLISHERS IN ORDINARY TO HER MAJESTY.

1898.

[*This story appeared previously in the weekly edition of " The Times."*]

THE MISCHIEF-MAKER.

CHAPTER I.

CUNNINGHAM'S sleep did not seem to have refreshed him, for he woke in a savage humour. He received the news of his visitor in silence, but when I mentioned Miss Green, an expression of distrust crept into his eyes as they met mine. It was plain to see he did not relish my acquaintance with his affairs, and he took no special pains to conceal his dislike of me. But though he seemed to me to be on the high-road to make an utter fool of himself, it was none of my business to lecture him.

Sutherland came late.

" I've been on the river," he said ; " that's why I didn't turn up this morning. I'm doing the sights, like any country cousin. I see you were round at Brown Street. What made you refuse to go to Mrs. Tom's ? "

" I suppose I was conceited enough to fancy I couldn't be spared. But, upon my word, I don't know—I think I've only succeeded in enraging him."

" That's nothing. It's part of a sick person's religion to hate his nurse. But you'll have to give up soon, you know ; you can't go on looking after him for ever, as if he was a baby in long clothes."

" He seems to be thinking of going away for change. But he's very down in the mouth."

" I'll talk to him," said Sutherland, with a smile ; " it's time somebody did."

If his feelings towards me were none of the warmest, Cunningham had still a wholesome respect for Sutherland. There was something in his very air and manner, cool and collected, that implied reserves of strength, and strength was of all things what the poor wretch most envied in the break-down of his nerves and morals."

"Go alone," I said, "I'll wait outside."

Sutherland nodded.

I lit my pipe and went out on the pavement, glad of the chance to draw a breath of fresh air.

It was a good bit before he joined me.

"I'm not much given to preachment," he said, "and I dare say I might as well have held my tongue. But neither you nor I can do anything more. It rests with Cunningham himself to finish his cure. If you've any influence over him, get him to leave town at once. He's healthy enough if he chooses to live cleanly and temperately, but his constitution won't stand the strain he's been putting on it of late. He should play cricket, or take to golf, and leave books alone for a while. I shan't come again unless you send for me. The sooner you get him off for your sake and his own the better."

At Cunningham's request I slept at his

lodgings that night, and to my surprise he asked me next day not to leave him. He made a shame-faced apology for his petulance, which it was easy enough to accept. He had been thinking over Sutherland's words in the night, and was bracing himself to make an effort after self-control. He asked for some of his papers, and lay staring at a half-finished manuscript which had been found on the table of the garret he occupied.

"I couldn't do that now," he said, looking at me rather piteously; "I couldn't put two sentences together, my mind's a blank."

"The power will come back. Suppose you read it aloud?"

It was a clever bit of writing, a review of a book of essays that had made some stir, touched with a lightness and brilliancy I had not given him credit for. It seemed possible that any one who could achieve so much might easily accomplish more.

He held out this hope for himself, when he said that he thought he would go out of London for the summer.

" There are bits of Hertfordshire and Bucks where the tripper is quite an unknown genus. I used to do some Saturday to Monday exploring when first I came south."

" It would be pretty dull for you, wouldn't it ? " I ventured. "Now, if you went north you could have company and quiet too."

" No, I shan't go north—yet," he said, with a tightening of his lips. "Shawbridge is a regular hole for gossip."

He said nothing of Mrs. Black's invitation to Finchley, and one was left to hope that in the saner view of himself and his affairs he was taking, he saw the unwisdom of running needlessly into temptation. He asked later in the day for pen and ink, and wrote two letters. One of them occupied him a long time. Perhaps it was humble, as it well might be ; sincere in such confession as it made, seeing it was written to the woman who had borne all things for his sake, and was faithful still.

On the following day we went for that postponed drive, choosing an hour when young Flower and his sister could go with us.

She was very bright and cheerful, and the invalid exerted himself to be cheerful too, as he sat on the back seat beside her. He was muffled up, and looked thin and white; but with a woman's tact she avoided all reference to his appearance. It was her brother who expatiated mournfully on the immense advantage the figure derived from a comfortable illness.

"Tom is afraid of growing stout," she said. "He's sure to be aldermanic when he's middle-aged, and that's against a doctor. Fat people, who wheeze when they walk, are never a bit impressive."

"A like fate will probably overtake you, miss," he retorted; "we come of the same stock."

"But in my case it won't matter," she said. "I dispense my advice like the oracles of old, from behind a veil."

"Are you to preside over the tea-cups all your life, then?" I asked.

"Who can tell?" she said, with a little

shrug of her pretty shoulders. "I only question the future for my clients. Let us put away business. What a pity it is we can't recognize our blessings while we have them! Here we are out for a holiday, and we're stupid enough to take our respective occupations with us. Here"—she made a little motion with her hands—"I'm going to throw the Tea-cup editress out of the carriage—there she goes— there's really no room for both of us; and Tom, if you import a single 'case' into the conversation, you shall be condemned to get out and walk home."

"All right; I suppose I may admire the pretty girls?"

"And what am I to think about?" asked Cunningham.

She turned on him with very womanly sweetness and gentleness.

"Think of the green fields and the blue skies you're going to," she said, "and the people who are waiting and rejoicing to think you're going to get well; think of all the beautiful conceptions and ideas that will come to you as you lie on the grass and get sunned through and through."

"Conceptions and ideas—that means pen and ink."

"That's shop," she said, with a warning finger. "Mr. Fowler is the only one of us who may employ his meditations on books and literary matters, because he's one of the useful general public who buy our wares."

Which constrained Mr. Fowler to announce that he intended forthwith to become a subscriber to the *Family Hearth*, and allow his views of life to be coloured by its sentiments.

We had not gone to the country after all; the country which yearly slips further and further from all encroaching London being somewhat hard to find. On our way to Regent's Park we were passing along a tree-bordered road, with glimpses of gardens making ready for spring. It was a quiet, unfrequented place, and two young people walking ahead of us seemed to have the side-path to themselves.

Looking at them with idle speculation, something struck me as strangely, disturbingly familiar in the man's walk. At that instant Miss Flower turned to me, and was on the point of an exclamation ; but, perhaps reading more than astonishment in my face, she had the tact to suppress it.

Neither of the others—they were in talk at the moment—noticed anything, but she and I knew it was Sutherland, and 1 alone that the girl at his side, tall and slim, who walked buoyantly, with an air of keeping pace with events was Miss Patricia Uniacke. It was an immediate relief to know that, engrossed with themselves, we had passed them unseen.

In the perplexed and perturbed condition of my thoughts one thing only was clear. Their very act of walking there unaccompanied had the binding force of a public confession. Miss Uniacke's friends at least would hold her pledged.

* * * * *

Cunningham's softened mood was a solace to me, since it gave me the excuse to be with him, helping forward his preparations for leaving town. For I found it impossible for the moment to face Sutherland. At the bottom of all my thoughts of him, and they were many and varied, was the sense of hurt that he had left me out of his confidences. We had been comrades so long, sharing all things, that his reticence now seemed the greater offence. Look back as I might on the last three weeks, I found no hint in them of his intention; no word that carried its warning of what was to come. Perhaps my own absorption was to blame; perhaps he was flung upon his fate with a precipitancy that left him no time to communicate his intentions. It was a queer business, and no explanation of it seemed the right one. Three weeks ago he had never set eyes on this girl, or so much as heard her name; three weeks ago his mind and heart were filled with the thought of some one else. Could one change so quickly as that?

Cunningham had to catch a train, so there came a moment when the last portmanteau was strapped. When rugs and bag had been tossed into the cab, Cunningham took his seat, and we shook hands; I watched him whisk round the corner with an odd sense of desolation. It had never before seemed possible that I should dislike him so little. I began to think I should miss him; with Sutherland absorbed in new interests the concluding days of our holiday offered no very lively prospect.

And now there was nothing to do but walk round to Brown Street. I had half hoped Sutherland might be out, but he was in; he stood smoking upon the hearth of our sitting-room with an air of meditating over matters.

He nodded good afternoon.

"Seen that young idiot off?" he asked.

"Yes."

I had brought an arm-load of books, and turned my back on him to arrange them on the shelf above the old-fashioned sideboard. Would he speak first?

"And a good riddance. You've played the Samaritan's part quite long enough, Harry."

"I dare say you've amused yourself better."

He made no reply. There only remained "Marcus Aurelius" and the "Confessions of an Opium Eater," to put up beside their neighbours. The books would have odd associations in the future, linking them with unquiet night watches; but at the moment I could only think of them as a shield between me and Sutherland. They made an excuse for speech without facing him.

"I saw you yesterday, at St. John's Wood."

My hand trembled, and "Marcus Aurelius" fell with a little clatter.

"Did you?" he said slowy. "Where were you?"

"Driving with Cunningham and the Flowers. We passed you and Miss Uniacke on the road."

"Yes," he said easily, "we were going to Herbert Spenceley's studio; he is Lady Uniacke's cousin."

I thought his behaviour intolerable; I wheeled round upon him, anger inspiring courage.

"Have you nothing to say?"

"I don't know that I have——" he was beginning, when a knock at the door interrupted him, and a moment later the land-lady announced Lord Mortlake. His red, embarrassed visage brought back in a flash that earlier interview at the station; he had the same air of helpless good temper, mixed with reluctant disapproval, that as good as advertised aloud his errand. Sutherland met him with a rather ironical smile. Evidently he had been in some measure prepared for this visit.

I went up to my room and sat miserably on the bed, picturing all that went on below.

The minutes ticked themselves very slowly till the door banged, and Sutherland sang out for me. He was standing where I had left him, and was relighting his cigar, which had gone out.

"You asked me half an hour ago if I had nothing to tell you, Fowler, and I said I didn't think I had; but half an hour has made all the difference. I'm going to marry Miss Uniacke."

"So I thought." For the life of me I could find nothing more to say.

He nodded.

"It won't be before summer; and of course it won't make any difference to you."

"Not to our friendship, I hope," I said, trying to hide from myself the vast difference it had already made.

"Nor to our comradeship; you'll stay on in the house."

"She might not like that."

"Oh yes, she will; and if she doesn't—why, then, she must." He put his hand on my shoulder for a moment, with a rare demonstration of affection that went to heal the sore in my heart.

And that was absolutely all either of us ever said about his engagement, though when I came to think of it I had not even congratulated him.

But here, let me tell those who did not know him, and who might misinterpret him as even I did in the first bewildered moments, his marriage was not the result of any foolish or light-minded flirtation. There are things which no man, if he is a gentleman, can say

even to his closest friend, and assuredly
Sutherland would never have told me that his
wife had begun to care for him before he had
given her a thought, except as a young girl for
whom he was rather sorry."

But that is simply how it all came about.
He was a good deal in Pont Street, graciously
urged to go—and in the intimacy that sprang
up, he could not but see that the mother and
daughter had little in common. Indeed, it
was a certain proud reserve under provocation
that first attracted Sutherland to Patricia. He
had no thought of being more than her friend,
kindly as it was his nature to be to any one
whom he held to be unjustly dealt by ; but for
all his clear-headedness he was no match for
the girl's mother, who was playing for her own
ends. Before he had been twice in the house
she had seen her own plan of action written
out clear, and schemed thereafter to make it
successful. Here was a young man of undeni-
ably good family, likely to rise in his profession, and whose home was in Scotland—a
comfortable distance from London—what if,

having met her under romantic circumstances, he should desire to marry Patricia? The match was as good as he could hope to make; it would help him in his career. As for Patricia, one knows what hero-worshippers girls are; it was plain to see that she had fallen in love with the partner of her adventures. Ladies who argue in this way do not always face the truth; but no doubt it lay in the back of Lady Uniacke's mind that a grown-up unmarried daughter would be quite a ridiculous blot on the bridal scene she had so often rehearsed. She had an exhaustless fund of youth, and power of enjoyment, which Patricia's presence only damped. After all, she was scarcely more than thirty-eight, and she looked ten years younger. So, with infinite tact, with a little push here and a little hint there, Sutherland was sent upon the prescribed path, and, being a man, never knew that he was guided. But, all the same, he might never have reached the goal of her desires, save for that involuntary betrayal on Patricia's part. Perhaps she could not keep the innocent meaning out of her eyes ; perhaps she broke down one day in tears. Enough that she stirred his pity and his chivalry so that affairs drifted onwards to that inevitable visit from Lord Mortlake, when Dr. Sutherland said he wished to request the honour of Miss Uniacke's hand.

And if anybody wants to know how I came to be acquainted with all these matters, I can only say that I have had frequent opportunities of being in Lady Mortlake's society, and that there is such a thing as arriving at the truth by an exhaustive process ; as for Sutherland's wife, she, as will be seen, has honoured me with a good many confidences, and even if she had withheld these, her transparent nature would confirm the truth of my guesses. So that this may be accepted as a perfectly veracious account of Sutherland's courtship and marriage.

He carried me off next day to pay my respects at Pont Street. Both ladies received me graciously. Patricia accepted my congratulations as calmly as if they were a

part of her everyday experience. I could
not help watching her with some amusement.
Happiness seemed to radiate from her; it
had a most extraordinary effect upon her
looks; the tired, frightened, rather thin and
immature young girl of the railway accident,
had bloomed into beauty; she had a little
air of dignity that was quite charming; she
was well dressed; it was worth while to
give her a new frock since she had so conveniently disposed of herself.

"Talk to him, Patricia," Archie said; "he's
got a ridiculous notion into his head that he
ought to leave us. Tell him he's behaving
absurdly."

"You are behaving absurdly," said Patricia,
with a little laugh. "I wouldn't have ventured on the criticism myself, for, you know,
I'm a little afraid of you, Mr. Fowler, but
when Archie says it, it must be true."

"He's by no means infallible, young as
he is," I answered; "and, in this case, I feel
sure Lady Uniacke will agree with me that
he is wrong."

"Your staying or going will not affect mamma," said Patricia, quietly; "we shall be four hundred miles apart from each other; Archie and I are the best judges, and we pronounce as your sentence that you continue to live in Hill Street till death us three do part, under pain of incurring our severest displeasure if you ever again hint at doing anything else."

"That's it," said Sutherland, laughing; "he's such a lady's man that he'll submit to anything rather than run the risk of displeasing you, Patricia."

"Oh, you'll both have something to put up with," she said, with a mock serious air. "I don't know anything about anything; I'm not a domestic character; I don't know how to bake or dust or mend; one would think I had been destined to marry a prince."

"You are talking very foolishly," said her mother, reddening angrily.

The girl bit her lip, and restrained herself.

"It remains that I'm an incapable," she

said; "but I'm willing to learn. Mr. Fowler shall teach me. I'm sure he knows the price of meat, and the different cuts, and the queer Scotch names. A leg of mutton is a gigot up there; I know that already. Is a leg of beef something else too?"

"Beef hasn't got any legs," said Sutherland; and we all laughed at the feeble pleasantry as we were perhaps meant to do to lighten the strain.

Lady Uniacke took me aside later on; indeed, we both squeezed ourselves into a tiny greenhouse on the stair landing, where she had conducted me on the plea of showing me her bulbs. She said I must see for myself how volatile and self-willed Patricia was, and I could guess what an anxiety she had been to a widowed mother; the poor child was at a sad disadvantage, brought up without a father's restraining hand.

I murmured something to the effect that she was getting a good husband.

"Ah, but for that, do you suppose I would have parted from her?" she said, with an affect of pathos that was very well done. "He is charming—quite charming; unfortunately, it is a poor match as far as worldly means go, but what is that compared with character? Lord Mortlake thinks it desirable that Dr. Sutherland should insure his life, as some small provision, you know, for his wife—in case—— In this uncertain life one can never tell what may ·happen! I mention this to you as I may not have an opportunity of broaching the subject to him to-day; and I know you haven't a secret from each other. How delightful that is! And, oh, by-the-by, dear Mr. Fowler, now that my foolish child cannot protest, let me assure you how *very* wise I think you are to decide on having your own separate establishment. Two is company, etc., and how specially true that is of marriage! Patricia thinks now that a joint household would answer; but these little arrangements generally turn out badly, don't they? And it's so much better not to make the experiment at all, than to make it and fail. You won't be running quite away from Shawbridge, will you?   Lord Mortlake and I"—she smiled, consciously——"hope to have a peep of dear Patricia as a matron, when we are in Scotland, and we should like to see something of you too."

I promised her gravely that I would not fly beyond her reach, should she honour Shawbridge with a visit.   Then we looked at the flowerpots, and I was told which of the green spikes would blossom into Lilium Auratum, and which into Lily of the Nile, in the autumn, for Lady Uniacke was nothing if she was not artistic, and carried out, quite perfectly, the pretence that we had come there for no other object.

Sutherland was displeased when I gave him her message, as we walked home together.

"I know perfectly what she's up to," he said.   "She's tried it on before.   Mortlake told me, privately, he meant to invest a sum for Patricia on her marriage, and her ladyship wants me to insure my life so that there won't be any need for his generosity.   She doesn't care that it should be extended to her daughter. But how can I afford the annual payment on £10,000 ? It's not to be done, even if I were convinced that insurance was the best kind of investment. There will be all sorts of extra expenses. I must have a new carriage for Patricia to use when she wants it.

"But her own money——"

"No," he said decisively, "I shan't touch a penny of that. I told Mortlake so. He's at liberty, of course, to do what he likes in the way of making provision for her. I've no right to object; but whatever she has must be settled on herself. I won't deny that it's a relief to know that her future is secured. If I leave her a young widow, she can get along very decently on what she has ; and if I live—well, she'll be none the worse off because I refuse to be dictated to by my mamma-in-law ; so don't you be beguiled into listening to any more of her nonsense."

"Could you be ready to go home next week, Harry ?" he said presently, in a casual sort of way.

"I suppose so. There's nothing to keep me here."

"It's before our time is up; but as I've to be back in June, I can't afford any more holidays."

"Is the wedding to be in June?" I asked, trying, not very successfully, to seem interested.

He nodded.

"We must get our second-class little affair over before the big event comes off. Mortlake and Lady Uniacke are to be married in the middle of the month. Fortunately, we shan't be expected to be present."

It was on the tip of my tongue to say that Lady Uniacke would also consider that a providential circumstance; but, seeing that she had probably arranged matters with a view to this end, it seemed a needless remark; so I said sapiently instead—

"There will be a good deal to do at home."

"Nothing that I know of—unless you think, with Mrs. Tom, that it is necessary to prepare Mrs. Laidlaw's mind."

"I dare say it's prepared already."

"How ? " he asked sharply.

"I told Frank Cunningham. I didn't suppose there was any secret about your engagement."

He looked at me frowningly for a moment, and then he nodded curtly; and I, who know him so well, knew that, upon reflection, he was rather relieved. It would have been embarrassing, to say the least of it, to be the bearer of his own news. For Mrs. Laidlaw's comments he cared not a straw; but there were others—there was one other who might think—— But what, after all, did it matter what she thought?

"There's the drawing-room. You'll have to furnish that," I reminded him.

" Eh ? Oh, well, a few chairs and tables, I suppose, is about all that's wanted! Patricia can add the fans and nicknacks women love. You could get the whole thing done while we're gone. You'd have a clear week."

" Is that to be the extent of your honeymoon ?"

"To my mind, it's a week too much. A

honeymoon's just the worst sort of mistake. It gives two idle people time to find out each other's weak points, and get heartily tired of each other before they've fairly made the experiment of living together. If Patricia had been a little older I would have suggested our going straight home, where we'd each have something to occupy us ; but a girl can't see beyond the romantic point of view."

"The modern girl can. You would like her view still less."

"Thank Heaven, Patricia isn't new-woman-ish," he said. "Of the two, her mother is nearer the type ; but I'm not going to marry my mother-in-law."

Being now an idle person at large, I went one day to see Mrs. Tom Carnegie. She was alone, the colonel having gone to the first spring meeting at Kempton Park. She looked older, to my eyes, with a hint of a line down her cheek and past her rounded chin—the line that comes to care-free women when middle life is reached, and to others who are less care-free a good deal earlier.

She received me with more kindness than I deserved, and spoke eagerly of Sutherland's engagement. She had called by Archie's desire on the household at Pont Street, and had struck up a little friendship with Patricia, taking the girl's part, as one could readily see, against the mother.

"Of course I know that there was some one else," she said suddenly, to my surprise and embarrassment. "Don't be afraid. I won't ask any indiscreet questions."

"But," I stammered, "what could make you think that?"

She smiled at my ignorance.

"He is not in love now," she said. "Perhaps he gave all that he has to give—perhaps he will waken up and begin to care again; and then you and I must pray that it will be his wife he falls in love with."

"Why, Sutherland is the last chap in the world to care for anybody else's wife," I said, feeling rather nettled. "You've got quite a wrong idea of him."

"Oh, I don't mean to suggest anything

melodramatic, or tragic, if you like the word better," she said. "I am sure he will always make quite an irreproachable husband, but he hasn't any foolish infatuation! He's 'like a prince royal. A woman asks for something more, you know, than polished manners. It isn't enough to have the door opened each time she goes out of the room, and her parcels carried, and her cloak put on, and her gloves buttoned. These things are very nice and charming, but they don't take the place of love. She would far rather her husband took the easiest chair himself, and neglected her in little ways, if she felt absolutely sure he couldn't do without her in big ones."

"I dare say Sutherland will unbend from his Prince Royal attitude in the privacy of domestic life; I'll report the first symptoms of neglect on his part. In the mean time I fancy it suits Miss Uniacke very well to be compassed with observances."

"She's so young," said Mrs. Tom, gently, "and of course it's a very wonderful thing to be engaged. She likes the promotion, and

she has had no kind of experience; that's one
thing for which she has to thank that horrid,
jealous mother of hers. At nineteen, most
girls in these days would have got to the end
of their emotions; but she's fresh to everything. Oh, I think she may be very happy,
if she never finds out."

"There is nothing to find out."

"Nothing, and yet everything. It all
depends. But I dare say she isn't sentimental;
and there will be her trousseau to interest her.
She will be immensely taken up with that,
and she won't miss—the other."

"It's consoling to know that you've found
her an alternative," I said, shaking hands.
"Now I can go home comforted."

As if one worry weren't enough, I was
destined that same week to have another
thrust upon me. I had left Archie in Bond
Street buying an engagement ring, and I was
going along in blind and absent fashion busy
with the problem of his future, when I was
startled to be suddenly accosted by a tall foot-
man, who paused in front of me.

"I beg your pardon, sir; but my mistress sent me to say she would be much obliged if you would speak to her."

"Your mistress!"

"Mrs. Black, of the 'All, Finchley, sir. The kerridge is waiting a little way down."

A little lower down accordingly I went, and soon discovered Mrs. Black's good-natured face anxiously scanning the moving throng; it lightened with satisfaction when she saw me.

"I recognized you as you went by," she said; "but I couldn't attract your attention. Can you spare me five minutes, Mr. Fowler? Won't you get in? Is there anywhere I can set you down?"

"Thanks. If Pont Street isn't out of your way?" I went round and got into the landau by the other door, sitting, by her request, in that seat I had last seen occupied by Miss Sophia Green. What a supercilious and offended air she had worn, with her uplifted nose and chin. The recollection made me ask for her.

"No, she's not with me," said Mrs. Black;

"she's gone home, and a good thing too, perhaps. It was that I wanted to talk to you about, for you were very good to Frank. Her father—Sophia's father—got word that she was corresponding with Frank Cunningham, and he came up and carried her off. Made her pack up and travel with him that very night back to Scotland. He was dreadfully angry, and Black and me, we didn't know how to pacify him. These quiet-like men, when they get into a temper, are worse than the hot ones."

"Do you mean that Miss Sophia and Cunningham have been writing to each other since he went into Hertfordshire?" I asked, thinking many bitter things of the graceless young scoundrel.

"Yes," she said; "and I never hindered it, like the old fool I am. But if you had seen them when they were both visiting us two years ago—he was so taken up with her music, and she thought it such a fine thing that he should write books and be noticed in the papers—it was as pretty as a picture to see them together. They seemed just made for each other—and young love is a good thing, you know, Mr. Fowler; it steadies a man, and spurs him on, too, and gives him an aim; and—and I never thought the idea would be unwelcome to Sophia's father. Green was just nobody, like a good many who have done well, and one wouldn't have thought he'd be so hard to please—for Frank is a clever lad, and well mannered, and well looking too."

Well mannered!

"Didn't you know," I asked, "that he has been engaged for years to some one who—who is not Miss Sophia?"

She turned a large startled face upon me, flushed deep with shocked shame.

"Not Frank!" she cried. "Don't tell me Frank could be so dishonourable! He seemed such an innocent laddie—like a boy of our own. Oh, surely he would never lead a girl on to care for him when he knew he couldn't marry her!" To the innocent lady with her simple code this seemed a disgraceful offence. Surely he must have broken off with the first, though that wasn't a very nice thing to do either, before he began to care for Sophia, for he did care for her, Mr. Fowler. I've seen too many young people not to be sure."

"His engagement certainly held good up to a week ago."

"Then all I can say is, I hope the poor young lady will never hear of his on-goings," she said fervently; "I don't know which to be most sorry for, her or Sophia."

"I don't think Miss Sophia's heart will break," I said; "I dare say she knew the rules of the game. Perhaps Cunningham felt he had had enough of it too, when he refused your invitation."

"Well, and I was as vexed as could be when he wrote to say he couldn't come, for I did hope it would be the beginning of a friendlier feeling on his part, and it would just have been a delight to me to look after Frank and coax him back to health. I don't know what Mr. Black will be saying, for he quite took a notion of Sophia, and he thought it very hard on a young lass to be carried off like that, and she up here for a little bit of pleasure. But nothing he said would move Benjamin Green; and off he went, with a face that would sour milk, scarcely giving the bairn time to pack her clothes, and scolding all the while."

"Perhaps a parental lecture would do her good," I ventured, but was sorry the next moment, for she turned on me a face of such genuine distress that not even the gorgeousness of her bonnet could temper its sincerity.

"You'll not tell me that she knew he was engaged!" she asked piteously. And I did not tell her; I perjured myself willingly for her peace. After all, I did not know for certain, and it was no business of mine to denounce Miss Sophia's pranks, or to grieve the heart of this kind woman.

"I don't think young people are what they were in my early days," she said plaintively; "they've lighter hearts, maybe, and they laugh where we should have cried. But I'm glad you think Sophia is innocent, and we'll just keep the matter to ourselves and never let a cheep of it come out, for a young girl's good name

is just everything to her, Mr. Fowler; it's just
her very life.   Her father will hold his tongue,
his hurt pride will keep him silent.   And,
maybe, as you say, Sophia won't be grieving
long, for from what Benjamin Green let out,
there's another lover in the wind, and we'll
just hope that no whisper of this will get the
length of the other young lady, to be disturbing
and vexing her, and then no great harm will
have been done."

I could not but admire the delicacy of
feeling that forbore to ask the name of
Frank's first love, but was it so sure that her
trust had been left unshaken?

"Do you know how Mr. Green heard of
this correspondence?" I asked.

" I couldn't rightly say," she replied; "but
I think he found out she had been getting
letters in the winter addressed to Mrs.
Laidlaw's."

Involuntarily, under my breath, I consigned
that mischief-maker to impolite quarters, and
covered the lapse with a cough as my companion turned towards me.

"I know you're calling her a meddlesome old woman; and so indeed would I. But what better am I myself?"

"No, no, never a Mrs. Laidlaw!"

"Well, I can't but blame myself all the same, for at my age I might have had more sense. Dear, dear, I hope no harm will come of it, and I'm very glad to have met you, Mr. Fowler, for you were very good to Frank, and it seemed only due to you to tell you, for when Sophia and I went to his lodgings and saw you, I thought it was all smooth between them, and a match likely to come of it some day. And I'm sure I'm grateful to you for listening so patiently, and next time you're in town—you're going north immediately, you say?—well, the next time, if you'll dine with us at Finchley, or spend a day or two with us, if you can put up with our homely ways, it will give my husband and me real pleasure."

CHAPTER II.

NEITHER the minister nor his study was at all changed—it was only we who had come back different. There was the same dust upon the musty books—broom or besom was rarely allowed here—a Father that had been placed upside-down in the middle row facing the fire still retained that ignominious position; only the yellow sermons had been turned, the bottom one to the top. It had a round ring upon it where a hot dish had reposed; it was of good things to eat and drink the air smacked, even though the window was open, and fragrant June outside.

"I am not uncharitable, I hope," said the minister, with pomposity; "I trust no man can lay that failing to my charge. But as a parent, Mr. Fowler, as a parent, I could have wished that it had fallen to some one else—to a stranger, to rescue that erring youth. Your connection with Shawbridge, your knowledge of his previous history, have all helped to revive feelings which I had hoped he had learned to overcome; which, for all concerned, it would have been advisable he should overcome."

He walked up and down the room, his dressing-gown flowing about him, a tassel from the unfastened girdle held in his white hand and used to emphasize his words.

" Why advisable ? " I asked.

He swung the tassel as if he would have hit me with it.

" Sir," he said violently, " I have a daughter ! "

I had never felt anything for him but a kind of amused contempt. I believe his feelings towards me were of much the same quality; but just then I pitied him. He was for the moment sincere. Down at the other Manse a blind man had groped till he reached and held my two hands in a nervous grasp. This was what he said—

" I won't thank you—I can't even try to thank you—for what you have done for my son; but you have had your reward already. It is a great privilege—the greatest, perhaps—to help a stumbling fellow-creature to stand sure again. A hand outstretched in time may make all the difference between salvation and eternal condemnation."

Such was the stern creed he held—the sad-faced, sweet-faced man with the sightless eyes.

That was the difference between the men; but then, the one had a son to save, and the other a daughter to sacrifice. How could they see eye to eye in this matter ?

Perhaps my sympathies were more on the side of Dr. Gillespie than they had been before that visit to town, and those night watches by a sick-bed. The minister's ambition was hurt by his daughter's choice, and his love, which was honest in its way, was hurt too. He would dearly have liked her to marry what men call well. Wasn't he excellently fitted to be the father of a wealthy lady? He loved the high places of this life, and felt himself genially suited to them. It was his secretly-cherished hope that he would one day be Moderator of the General Assembly. And yet he was asked to accept as his son this disreputable penny-a-liner, brought up within the pale of the Free Kirk; an advocate of disestablishment—a red-hot radical or socialist, for all he knew.

This last to me, while he paced the room—too big for it. His bulk and breadth, which with the passage of time were gaining coarseness, showed to best advantage in the open air.

"I don't think he bothers himself much about politics—few literary men do."

"Literature!" said the doctor, with a snort. Seeing that he did not even write his own sermons, he naturally thought poorly of it as a trade.

"It's looking up in the world," I said, to cheer him. "A prominent novelist was knighted the other day—actually knighted, like any prosperous retired grocer. It is being recognized as a respectable calling; it is even being paid for—moderately, very moderately ; people who only amuse their neighbours mustn't expect too much. It is felt that they ought to be very thankful to be allowed to live. They are even protected in a measure from forcible robbery of their wares. They and all the tribe of creative folk are beginning to have a better time of it. Do you remember how Mr. Clive Newcome was looked down on and wondered at because he chose to be an artist, and Mr. Pendennis as a journalist was considered scarcely more respectable ? "

"I never read fiction," said the minister, speaking as one who is proud of himself. Indeed, he never read anything but the *Shawbridge Herald.*

" There is one thing you ought to read, sir : Frank Cunningham's article in the Bi-Weekly ; it is full of cleverness and freshness. It has already attracted notice, and is sure to make its mark."

" Why should I read it ? " he asked irritably. "Will it make him forget my daughter? Will it make her think less of him ? "

"It will materially help him to improve his position. A story-writer must bide his time, and the chances of public favour; but a clever journalist can command his own prices."

The minister turned on me a passionate, purple face. He allowed an expression to escape him which may be left unrecorded; it was unministerial, but I never liked the man half so well as when he swore at me, and cried out—

"D'ye think I want the fellow to succeed?"

He was honest enough for once.

He left the room abruptly. When he was ruffled it soothed him best to go among his people, where there was plenty of incense burned before him. Pastoral visitation became a fine art in his hands. In one house he would examine the children upon the Shorter Catechism, skipping the proofs, and lenient towards mistakes; he would even pray with their elders, using a form that varied little, and was supposed to cover all human needs; in another, a genial jest seemed more appropriate. He was at one, too, with the old Selkirk divine who thought that a minister should practise with discretion the taking of a little spirits, not to affront a parishioner's hospitality.

In most places he was a favourite, his portly bigness was ornamental; it was a pleasure to shake that white hand, with the carefully-kept nails; his bland suavity was as oil to the friction of life. At home he had a daughter who opposed him; among his flock he was king and dictator. Short-bread and "sherry-wine" were pressed upon him; the bairn's faces were scoured before they put on bashful smiles in his presence. All the tit-bits of news, the delicacies of gossip, were reserved for his ear. He liked this best.

Shaved and punctiliously dressed in clerical attire, I had watched him—with his air of not at all desiring to think himself more important than other people—walk down the road, where, ten minutes later, Nancy and I followed.

I had been waiting for her, while she went to the other Manse to gather certain roses which she held to be more fragrant than any in her own garden, and we were on our way to decorate the house in South Place for the arrival of the Sutherlands.

She seemed to me to have grown a little graver than before, but her recent experiences had been disquieting, and there had been, I knew, some kind of explanation with her father, which had left him displeased.

I wondered how much she knew—or guessed—about Cunningham's illness, and hoped she would not question me, but she did.

"I have not asked you before," she said, "because there has not been an opportunity,"—we had not been alone till now—"but I hope you will tell me; I feel that you are my friend."

"Indeed I am."

"You have proved it, and will prove it again in being quite frank with me. It is best that I should know."

If she was strong enough to bear it, perhaps it was best. If I doubted still, there was something in her waiting silence that compelled me.

I told her, leaving nothing out.

We continued to walk upon the road, past the graveyard where her mother slept—she may have wished for her mother then—and the garden-circled villas, set closer to each other as we neared the entrance to Shaw Street. She had a sunshade over her shoulder, and for one moment I thought it quivered in her hand, but she kept step with me, looking straight before her. What did she see? How much in that moment did she renounce? How much did she understand? How much can any woman, who is pure, understand of the deeps to which a man may fall? She had bared her breast to the wound, but I was not to see how it ached.

"Thank you," she said at last; "and now I will tell you why I wished to know. I think it likely we may be married before long."

It had been hard to obey her, but this

was too much. I had known all along that she would marry him, yet never fully realised it till now. My whole soul rebelled within me; cried out in fierce protest against this useless sacrifice. In some roughly-chosen, unguarded words, I said as much to her.

My vehemence perplexed and surprised her; but she thought a moment, and then said gently—

"Each person's course of action is, or ought to be, a part of himself; you would not have me unfaithful to my own belief in what is best, would you?"

"But one's belief depends so much on one's point of view. What seems a duty looked at close, may not be one at all if one could survey it from a distance. It is a safeguard to put one's self outside of one's self."

"I do not agree with you; right must be right, from whatever angle one surveys it. And if one recognizes something as a duty, why should one wish to safeguard one's self against it because it may possibly entail suffering? Isn't that to be a coward?"

"We have all a right to happiness."

She looked at me wistfully.

"Happiness means such different things to different people," she said, with a smile; "it is one of those clumsy generalizations we use to cover an infinite variety of emotions. There is no love which is quite perfect, but there are some of us who would rather have the love we want, with all its imperfections, than a relationship that better satisfied the world's theories, but left our sympathies untouched. Oh, I am not good at arguing. One can feel, but one cannot find words. But I have cared for Frank since we were little together, and that makes a binding tie; it makes faithlessness impossible."

"Such faithfulness should raise a man to his highest."

"And if he needs me—if he is weak and can use my strength," she said, her eyes alight with steadfast purpose, "surely that is a reason the more why I should cling to him? One would be a poor and pitiful kind of creature if one could only care when the sun shone and things went well, and turn one's back when the dark days came. If we were more patient—if we were a little truer to each other—there wouldn't be half the misery or the wickedness there is in the world. We go wrong because some one has failed us. A little trust, surely, is worth while."

I thought of the minister's words. Strange efficacy of human sympathy—could it indeed work miracles? Could it turn low aims into high ones—indolence into strength, folly into wisdom? It was much to ask, even of so divine a thing as a woman's love.

"I'm afraid you think me either very visionary or pitifully conceited," she said, after a pause. "Perhaps I am wrong. I may over-rate my own strength, there are others who think so," she sighed; "but then, does another person's view ever really help us? I have always thought that the only right that is worth anything to us is the right we arrive at by ourselves."

"Isn't that rather mutinous doctrine? What

becomes of the accumulated experience of the ages ?"

"I don't know," she laughed; "but it doesn't seem to have made the world very much wiser. Every age demands its own teachers, and every individual must, in the end, be a lawgiver to himself. But how grave we have been, and how I must have bored you! Let us talk of something else."

It could not bore me that she should think fit to give me her confidence. And for herself, she was happy in that the vision lifted before her eyes had for her an authority she could not disobey, and was strong enough to accept willingly.

She was quite genuinely interested in Sutherland's courtship. I had thought that, to so proud a nature, there would have been some affront in his speedy choice of a new love; but no such feeling was betrayed. It was her own proposal that she should look over the rooms I had striven to put in order, and add those little touches that can only be given by a woman's hand.

Burton admitted us with a glour on his brow that showed how he was "hauding himself in." His master's marriage had been a sore trial to Burton, and only his attachment to ourselves and the house made it endurable. Indeed, he had announced that his stay was conditional; little did Patricia guess how severely her actions were to be scrutinized, how keenly judged. In Burton's eyes all women were "trash," not worth a man's "fash"—an all-ruling Providence might surely have contrived a world without them.

"How pretty you have made this room," said Nancy, heartily. She was standing in the bow window where Burton's geraniums had sunned themselves; I could think of nothing but the strangeness of seeing her there, where, had she chosen, she might have reigned mistress.

"You really think so? Sutherland would give me no help. He always declares he has no ideas, yet he can very sharply criticize anything he does not like."

"He will find nothing, or very little, to

criticize here. I suppose this is London taste. It is like a June sky at the gloaming. There is certainly not another amber and white room in Shawbridge."

"It's the nearest substitute for sunshine, and a room with only one window is apt to be dull ; but I had qualms over the carpet. I hope Patricia will like it."

"Patricia—it's a high-sounding name, isn't it ? I like these mouth-filling names, such as Honoria, Antonia, Valeria—you can't debase them by cutting them down into silly diminutives ; there's a kind of distinction about them that one would feel compelled to live up to."

"I believe Lord Mortlake, her stepfather, sometimes enrages her by calling her Pat. He has known her ever since she was a child, and he is one of those good-natured people who think you must feel hurt unless they are occasionally familiar—a nickname is a species of caress with them."

"And such a nickname ! It is only with a homely name like mine that you can safely take liberties."

"What is your real name?"

"I was christened Nancy," she was beginning, when a loud knock at the door startled us both.

"An importunate visitor."

"Some one for the assistant."

But Burton's face told another tale.

"Mrs. Laidlaw, sir; and she wants to see you."

We looked at each other in blank dismay.

"Couldn't she have chosen some other day? She hates me, you know!"

"Tell her I'm engaged, Burton."

He continued to wait, the door-handle in his hand, a frown upon his brow, his mouth set doggedly.

"I could pitch Andra Souttar, the shauchlin' body, out on the road as easy as look at him," he said, "but yon muckle wife in the wheel chair—she's a different story."

Nancy laughed.

"It's useless to rebel," she said. "You will go out, and she will come in, and she will want to see this room, and you'll have to bring her in."

"You won't go?"

"No," she said, with a hint of pride; "there is no reason why I should run away because Mrs. Laidlaw calls. I will stay and support you; and, in the mean time, if Burton will be so kind as to bring me the glasses, I'll put those roses in water."

Mrs. Laidlaw had emerged from her chair, and was labouring up the steps, supported on one side by Andrew Souttar, and on the other by the meek McAlister. Each flat foot as it was placed on a succeeding step seemed to proclaim its conquest over new territory.

"Well," she said, when she stood on the oilcloth and had recovered breath, "fine doings ye've been having, I hear, making a Shirra Muir of the place. I've come to see what ye've been about. McAlister, you can bide out-bye."

"Excuse me," I said, "but for the present at least I am master here. Burton, show Miss McAlister into the drawing-room."

She looked at me with timid gratitude.

"You'll find Miss Gillespie there," I added,

to encourage her ; " she'll be glad of your help to arrange some flowers. Mrs. Laidlaw, will you please come into the dining-room ? "

She surveyed me grimly, as if she would have annihilated me ; but, thinking better of it, said, with a kind of boisterous jocularity—

" We're all to do as we're bid, it seems, as meek and mum as ye like. Well, it's but a short day ye'll play the master, my bonnie man ! "

" So short that, as you see, I'm abusing my privileges. There's a comfortable armchair here, Mrs. Laidlaw."

" Hoots," she said, but letting herself be led forward, " ye can't so easy get on my blind side as all that. Why don't ye own at once you're feared I'll find out Nancy Gillespie is here ? "

" How can I be afraid of that when I have just told you she is here ? And why should I be afraid ? "

" There was no need to tell it," she said significantly, " for I knew it already ; that's why I came."

Now, if I were not the most blundering of chroniclers, I should have told before this of a weapon that had been put into my hand to use, if need be, against this adversary. It came into my possession thus. When we were about to leave London, Sutherland was suddenly detained by business connected with his marriage for one day longer. Having nothing to do with this affair, and time hanging heavy, I bethought me of Mrs. Black's invitation, and went to call on her at Finchley. She received me warmly, but was still troubled, as I could see, about this matter of Frank Cunningham and Sophia Green. She invited me to sit with her, in a delightfully-sheltered verandah, and, looking down the cool spaces of lawn and border, she said, after a long silence—

"Mr. Fowler, I am going to tell you something about Mrs. Laidlaw. I have thought of it ever since I last saw you, wondering what it was right to do, and to see you here seems to be an answer to my doubts. I am not a malicious woman, I hope, and gossip I abhor, but Mrs. Laidlaw has been encouraging Sophia, and she will make mischief now that she is crossed. I know what she is if she does not get her own way; she will colour this story, and make a foolish flirtation into something much more serious—something that will hurt another person, unless you can stop her."

"I? I don't want to have anything to do with her," I said, with profound distaste. "I can't abide her."

"But you have been helping Frank, and—if you can help the woman who loves him?"

Ah, she did not know how strong a plea she used!

"Tell me, then, if you think it best."

"What I am going to make known to you will stop her from spreading any idle tales, because she will be afraid of you. I trust to your honour to tell no one else, and not to let her know you know unless you must."

I promised, and she told me.

That was why I decoyed the woman who hated Nancy Gillespie into the dining-room.

"Mrs. Laidlaw," I said, taking the bull by the horns, "you are aware, I believe, that there has been some boy-and-girl nonsense between Frank Cunningham and Sophia Green?"

"Deary me! So you've been playing the go-between, have you?" she said, affecting surprise. "I mind now, ye looket after the lad when he was ill, and much beholden we all were to you. And so he let you into his mind, did he? Well, and why not? Not that you're the kind to take a lassie's fancy yourself, but that's neither here nor there. It's the old maids that hear the most love-stories, and I dare say the bachelors get their share of confidences too. And now that I can count on your powerful help, Mr. Companion—for we know fine that you're always on the side of the oppressed—between us we'll maybe laugh in our sleeve at Bengy Green, and make a match of it yet."

"We'll do nothing of the kind," I said, repudiating this partnership; "you know, as well as I do, that it was all a piece of childish, unthinking folly, and that nothing ever would have come, or was ever meant to come, of it.

Young people amuse themselves with these
little rehearsals to keep themselves in practice.
I dare say you did it yourself, in your young
days."

"What is it you would be at?" she asked
sharply. "You didn't wile me in here to
talk of my young days, I'll warrant. Are ye
in love with Sophia yourself?"

"Heaven forbid! I'm only in love with
peace, and it seems to me it would be best
gained if we all held our tongues over this
silly flirtation. Shawbridge knows, and need
know nothing if we are discreet. Mr. Green
has been wise enough to treat it with the
contempt it deserves, and I hear Miss Sophia
is provided with a real lover——"

"And is it Benjamin Green's feelings you're
so set on sparing? He ought to be beholden
to ye. Man!" she cried, her eyes suddenly
blazing, "d'ye think I'm a doited fool that
I can't see through ye, and read ye like a
book? It's Nancy Gillespie you're set on
shielding; it's her precious feelings we're all
to consider, keeping a calm sough so that

never a breath of yon feckless lad's folly and his fickleness and his veecious courses may reach her ears! Ye expect me—me that she's flouted and defied—to spare her! Ye think, maybe, I cared that yon little hizzy should mate with young Cunningham? What is Green's daughter to me that I should fash myself over her or her light loves, but that it gave me a chance to spite Nancy Gillespie and bring down her pride? If ye think to talk me over, ye may save your breath for some better purpose. I'll go my own ways without asking your pleasure, or hers either. Ye're over-ready to meddle, and you're not over-wise; but though ye can cross no plan of mine, it's maybe as well to remind you that *I* rule in Shawbridge. And that's the last word that need be said. Come away with ye, and let me see what extravagance you've been leading the doctor into. You and me needn't be falling out—and you'll be wise if you keep Jennet Laidlaw your friend."

" Only on one condition will I accept your friendship."

"And who are you to make condections?" she asked stormily.

"A very insignificant person; but, as it happens, I am in possession of some knowledge concerning yourself that you would not like to be made public property. A threat is an ugly thing, a low thing, maybe, but you force me to use your own weapons. Unless you promise silence on this matter, I will repeat what I know to be the true history of the sale of Grainger's Mill."

She looked at me with a face of passionate disdain, as if I were a thing almost too small for her contempt, and it was easy to believe that no one had ever before ventured to thwart her. Probably no one had ever had sufficient motive, for all remembrance of the disreputable transaction to which I had alluded was supposed to be buried in the wronged man's grave.

"A likely tale!" she said at last, affecting mirth; "and to whom will ye carry this fine, made-up story?"

"To Mr. Horace Little," I said, without premeditation; "he is an honourable man."

" You are a fool to cross me ; as I've told ye already," she said, " I'm an ill woman to thwart ; " but she rose, and I knew that I had won. " You had better have made an enemy of any man or woman in Shawbridge than of me ; there's little comfort for anybody here that's in my black books, let me tell ye," she said, with a belief in her supremacy that was really fine in its way.

" Perhaps," I said, " though I don't see what harm you can do me. Anyway, I'll take the risk. I don't want to quarrel with you or with anybody ; you've only got to infuse a little discretion into your talk, or to leave a certain subject out of it, and you will find I can be silent too."

" Muckle I care for your silence ! Send the town-crier round with your news, Mr. Tale-pyet : who'll believe your word against mine ? Answer me that ! Me, that has lived in Shawbridge, respectet and looked up to, the best of my days, or you, an orra tyke, with your bit bark that frichtens naebody but yoursel' ! "

"Don't count too surely on your neighbours' charity," I said; "you haven't shown them so much that they will be ready to make excuses for you. And most people love a bit of scandal and believe in it too."

It was not very dignified to be bandying words with her; but she was a detestable old woman, and she deserved the only sort of punishment she could feel. Loss of prestige in the little town where she had made herself feared and obeyed would touch her to the quick. She was too proud or too cunning to ask me directly where I got my information, though it was plain that she burned to know. It was her cue to treat my threat as if it were a thing beneath her contempt, and I, a malignant and meddlesome fool, impotent to harm her; but I am glad to think that she never, in all her suspicions, lit on the right person. Good Mrs. Black, who suffered much in her conscience, and could never be sure whether she had done right or wrong in arming me with this weapon, was at least spared the exhibition of spite and malice reserved for me until Shawbridge and its reigning lady were left behind and forgotten.

" Are you a magician ? " asked Nancy, when I went back to the drawing-room, " that you have rid us so easily of the ogress ? That poor little woman was quite frightened when you sent Burton for her. Her first thought was that her mistress must be dead."

" I'm afraid there's a bad quarter of an hour in store for her; Mrs. Laidlaw isn't in an amiable humour. What an improvement your flowers are to the room."

" Haven't we been diligent ? But you haven't told me how you routed Mrs. Laidlaw."

" Oh, she was easily disarmed; she was wise enough to understand she wasn't wanted. When you've finished tea, will you go over the other rooms and tell me if there's anything I've forgotten ? "

Her roses were still fresh when Sutherland and his bride came home. They had kept strictly to the week of holiday-making, and to instructed eyes it was plain to see that he at least had found it long enough. There were arrears of work awaiting him, and he got into harness a trifle too eagerly, perhaps, for Patricia's contentment.

Poor child, it was hard she should find a rival already, and she but an eight days' bride. When Sutherland was with her he was all kindness and attention; he amused himself with her as if she were a clever and attractive plaything; but she had to learn, as I had had to learn long ago, that everything must give way to duty. How it might have been had he loved her, I do not know. But there was no temptation in his affection for Patricia.

She bore herself in the main gaily, however, taking an immense pride and pleasure in setting her home in order, and unpacking her innumerable wedding presents. An accidental meeting with Nancy, her first acquaintance in Shawbridge, was the beginning of a mutual attraction that soon led to a firm friendship between the girls. Each found something in the other that met a need. There were many reasons why Nancy should be unpopular in

Shawbridge. She was handsomer than most of the young women there—a sufficient justification of feminine coldness; her qualities of mind were equally disconcerting; her shrewdness had a tinge of sarcasm, and her humour was apt to ripple out at the vagaries of others as well as her own. Worst offence of all, perhaps, in a community where a substantial "downsetting" was the ideal kept steadily before the young folk, she had bestowed her affections unwisely on a young man who had nothing but a picturesque outside to recommend him. So that for her, Patricia's spontaneous gaiety and impulsive warmth had the greatest charm.

As for Patricia, she had, of course, had no time to taste the quality of the Shawbridge maidens when she chose Nancy to be her friend; but she, no less than the other, had had a lonely youth, and was prepared to hail a kindred spirit when it came within speaking distance.

"I suppose properly-married people—quite newly-married ones at least—shouldn't want girl friends?" she said tentatively to Sutherland that evening when he had given himself a quarter of an hour for an after-dinner smoke in the garden.

"I can answer for myself that they shouldn't," he replied, feeling amused at her serious air. "I find a girl-wife quite enough."

"But we are speaking of *me*, dear. Of course it would be quite improper for you. Do you think I would permit it? You have Friend Fowler for your Fidus Achates. And what can you want more?"

"Can a woman content herself with one bosom friend?" he asked sceptically.

"Why not?" she questioned haughtily.

"Varium et mutabile semper," he murmured. "You shall instruct me better. Who is the lady of your choice?"

I trembled for the pronouncement of the name. The light was beginning to pale a little—enough to hide subtleties of expression; Sutherland stooped to knock the ashes from his pipe; his tone to any other ear but mine would have seemed quietly natural when he said—

"You couldn't have chosen a better."

"Of course," said Patricia, "it would have been more satisfactory still if she had been married; then our sympathy would have been quite perfect : we could have discussed our husbands' little failings, tobacco, for instance, and a love of accumulating newspapers ; but, after all, it is only a question of time. She is engaged, I believe."

"Has she told you that—already ? "

"Indeed she has not!" said Patricia, indignantly. "Do you suppose I should like her if she rushed at me with a confidence like that in the first five minutes, and in a shop, too! There's nothing so detestable as gush."

"Then a revelation of that nature requires a special setting ? " he said, making an effort to speak jestingly. " Women are understood to unbosom themselves to each other while they're brushing their hair, I believe ? The reason why men are less confiding is, I suppose, because fashion allows them so little hair to brush."

"If she had button-holed me with an announcement like that, I should have thought it simply indecent," she went on, ignoring the interruption. "She shall tell me at her own time and in her own way; but I suppose "— she bent back in her seat to look at me— "you really had authority for making that statement?"

"The best authority."

"Then how funny that you haven't heard of it, Archie!"

"Are you not, perhaps, assuming too much?"

"Oh, to think you should hide things from your own wife! This is dreadful! If I had known you were a secretive person, I should have said 'Na,' like the lady of Cockpen's choice."

"Repentance comes too late," he said, getting up and pushing back his chair.

"You endowed me at the altar with all your possessions. That, certainly, includes a latch-key to your mind."

"A doctor's mind," he said, "is like a solicitor's deed-box—it's constructed to be the repository of other people's private concerns."

"I don't believe a lawyer has any mental reservations—towards Mrs. Lawyer," she said plaintively.

"Speech," he retorted, "was bestowed on a 'writer-body' to disguise his meaning. He does it to perfection—on paper—at a fee of six and eightpence."

They wandered away towards the house, she holding her skirts with one hand, the other thrust through his arm. In a last fragment of his talk that came back to me, he was upbraiding her for the thinness of slippers not calculated to withstand the heavy dew. He was doing it with vigour, and, I fancy, with relief, that he had steered her thoughts into new channels.

Poor child, there was for her no familiar running in and out among her husband's thoughts, and better not if she were to remain the carelessly playful girl she now was. In the isolation in which each of us lives and moves and suffers, lies the true pathos of life.

It was, of course, inevitable that Sutherland and Nancy should meet. So far as I could judge, she greeted him without a shadow of embarrassed feeling—with nothing but a kind and sisterly cordiality. She was entirely without paltry vanity, and might readily suppose that he had mistaken the strength of his attachment for her, and had now found the woman who suited him better.

A man's conceit is made of robuster stuff, and perhaps he would have preferred some sign from her that she had not totally forgotten the past. He betrayed that he still remembered it by avoiding her whenever he could, and behaving, when in her company, with a guarded politeness which rarely melted into the old friendliness. He could not shake off disturbing memories. If he had hoped that the marriage ceremony would act as a kind of spell or charm, blotting out the past, and creating a new mental attitude towards the future, he was no wiser than other men who have eagerly tried the same experiment, only to find it fail them. But Sutherland had a conscience, and he determined that his own mistakes—though he was far from admitting that he had blundered—should at least react on no one else. His work absorbed all but the fragments of his time, and in these he was always ready to give himself up to Patricia's whims. He showed that she was in his thoughts in a hundred little ways, of which any young wife might be proud. He was careful of her, indulgent, good-humouredly patient; and for the early months of her marriage at least she was entirely happy.

CHAPTER III.

WHEN there was nobody else to go about with her, Patricia had me at her beck and call. In one of our first walks in Shawbridge, she gave me a flattering proof of her regard.

"I have found a name for you," she said.

"I notice that I have been nameless hitherto. Do you object to my parents' choice?"

"Henry," she said slowly, as if she were tasting its quality. "The Henrys in English history weren't particularly meritorious, and the Henrys in fiction are mostly prigs. There was Henry in the 'Fairchild Family,' who was always getting into scrapes and repenting with unction, and the Henry who had a Bearer, and who died young because he was too good to live."

"That can't happen to me; though, to be sure, I can still be a grown-up prig."

"Do you know"—she looked at me with mischief in her eyes—"I'm sometimes afraid you have the least little bit of a tendency that way, and that's why I won't encourage you by calling you Henry. As for Fowler—Mr. Fowler—at the risk of being very rude, I do think it's extremely ugly."

"Unfortunately, I haven't your privilege of changing it. That's a woman's right that's denied to mere man."

"Unless you marry an heiress."

"Unless I marry an heiress. In the mean time, till she turns up, there's Harry left. Any objection to that?"

"That's Archie's name for you. I'm going to have one of my own; I'm going to call you Friend."

"Thank you," I said; "if we weren't in Shaw Street, where everybody to a certainty is peeping at us from behind the blinds, I would take off my hat to you for the honour you have done me."

"Never mind your hat. I'm glad you like my choice. There's something Quakerish—a trifle prim—about it, and you know you *are* a little old fashioned—I am going to cure you of that, Friend Fowler; but it's what I should like somebody whom I respected and liked to call me, so I hope you really think it's nice. You've been Archie's friend so long that I've a sort of right, now that I belong to him, to call you mine, haven't I ?"

" Every right, and I hope you'll never feel that I've ceased to deserve the grace you have bestowed."

" That's what I like about you," she said, confidingly, "those Sir Walter Raleigh speeches you make ; they're so refreshing in an off-hand age. I feel an inch taller, and I love to feel of importance ! "

Now and again she would pay me a visit in my high eerie, and I knew to put aside my reading when I heard her flying foot and quick tap at the door.

She would bring a fragment of sewing with her—a tangle of bright-coloured skeins and gold braid, or oftener, as a duster, a silk handkerchief purloined from Sutherland's drawer, which she proposed to use upon my shelves.

Like all unbookish women, she was an enemy to peaceful dust, and loved symmetry before all things. My favourites must needs herd in such order as she chose to place them, assorted in sizes and colours, and pulled to the very edges of the shelves, like soldiers on parade. It hurt me in the inward parts of me to see my trusted friends thus marshalled in incongruous battalions, and flicked about the ears with that too energetic handkerchief.

"How would you like to be paired off at one of your tea-drinkings," I remonstrated, " and compelled to neighbour a woman for no other reason than that she was the same height as you, and wore a gown of a like colour ?"

"I should feel that at least we had two things to sympathize about," she retorted. "There's more in being the same height than you think. You start fair; you need neither look down nor up. And of course, if she had the same taste in frocks, she would certainly be nice."

"But my books don't choose the fashion of their garments," I said; "and you classify them by their outsides, though they haven't a thought in common. You'll be cutting them down next to get them all on one level."

"They would certainly look neater," she said demurely.

"Neater!"

"Don't annihilate me; I'm beginning to shrivel already. You value your books, I dare say, for what's inside them; but you might remember that heaps of people, who would never want to open one of them, get a certain æsthetic pleasure from them simply as decorative wall furnishing."

"I can readily believe it."

"Now don't be sarcastic, for that's forbidden. You wouldn't have a new paper here, I don't know why, for this one is simply hideous; but since you took the doors off these nursery cupboards, and used the shelving, the room looks twice as well. But when I want to get the best effect out of the reds and blues, you go and push all the ragged and tattered poor relations right to the front, where they're nothing but an offence."

But how can a woman, who has a thousand occupations and little cares and pleasures and vanities and projected plans to occupy her, understand what a solitary man's books are to him? Friendlier than his pipe, more familiar than the stick that moulds itself to his palm with daily use, they wear the countenances of year-long housemates, each with its own honest features ready to kindle in greeting ; loved for the mere outer, human kind of look of it, that goes bail for the sparkle of its inner wit, or the quality of its humour. A book may wait years before its chance comes to reveal its message, with never a word of reproach for neglect ; but in the dark of a sleepless night, you can grope along the shelf and know it at a touch, without so much as striking a match, and count on its solace or its cheer. And to think that a meddlesome duster can bring chaos into this paradise of assured pleasure ;

divorce loving couples who have long rubbed shoulders, and part friends of a lifetime !

But to defend one's veterans to a woman is to waste good breath. Their rags, the thumb-marks and dog-ears of honourable service, offend her nice sense; while to their owner they only tell of years of faithful devotion, like the wrinkles on an old servant's face, making it the more lovable if less comely.

Patricia and I patched up a peace, and the silk handkerchief was waved no more, except as a flag of truce. As yet, there was a kind of radiance about her life, a sunniness which nothing had seriously disturbed. When Nancy went to Edinburgh, Patricia came to me with the small matters upon which her mind ran. She was in love with her destiny still, and had a girl's laugh for the little mischances that only gave happiness a finer edge.

The world of Shawbridge had called on her, and she was now returning its civilities. She was everywhere received with some ceremony, for, after all, we all love a lord, and Patricia's pedigree had an ornament or two of that nature. Rumour had given Mortlake fabulous wealth, though his purse was no more than very comfortably lined, and to be rich and aristocratic in a breath is a thing that may touch the dullest fancy. And, with this second-hand halo about her, Patricia moved in a royal sort of way; tongues stopping when she came in, and eyes quick to observe the costly simplicity of her dress, and the way she cocked up her head, and the ease of her manners. Her accent, as well as her antecedents made a subtle barrier; the broad northern burr had the sound of a foreigner's broken English in her ears; it gave her an amused sense of being in a new world; it smacked of travel. She grew to expect, as an opening question, after the weather had been pronounced "soft" or otherwise discussed and forsaken as a topic— "And how do you like living in Scotland?"

"And they look as if they dared me to say I didn't. What happens to people who don't like your country, Friend Fowler?"

"They are conducted to the Border, and banished forth of it for evermore."

"And they call that a punishment!" she said, half under her breath. "Pray, if you love your country so much, why are you all so anxious to leave it? I put that question to Mr. Horace Little the other day, between the bites of a cress sandwich, and he had the hardihood to tell me that Flodden was not yet avenged!"

"Your argument, madam, cuts two ways. If you hadn't been eating a cress sand-wich——"

"I'm so sick of shortbread!" she murmured.

"And no doubt, looking much too charming for serious treatment, Mr. Little might have asked what you were doing here?"

"Do you know, I sometimes ask myself that?" she said, twinkling. "I feel like a traveller without a road-map, wandering in a country where there are no signboards. And Archie won't help me one little scrap. I call it mean. He says I must form my own conclusions; and then, when I do form them, and propose to give him the benefit, he says I'm uncharitable. Now, isn't that illogical? I know what you'll say," she went on, without giving me an opportunity to say it; "you'll tell me he can't speak out because he's a doctor."

"Well, there may be some truth in that; he has to be careful, you see."

"I think that's so absurd! It makes him the slave of his patients."

"He can avenge himself when it comes to the prescription."

"He isn't small-minded," she fired up, with a flush of pride in him that was pretty to see. Why wasn't he there to see it?

"Nor is he altogether a meek, downtrodden worm."

"I think he ought to tell me his real opinion," she said, skipping back with a woman's agility to her first grievance. "I shouldn't proclaim it from the housetops, but I know those people must bore him."

"Well, a doctor must learn to be bored; that's part of his training."

"Must his wife be disciplined too?" she said, with a laugh. "It's a terrible thing to marry a profession. You've to treat it with such gingerly respect, as if it were a cut finger, that would make you feel it if you were the least bit careless, or touched anything too roughly. And"—she looked at me, her face changing a little, in mockery of herself—"I was goose enough to think I could help him!"

"Of course you can." There was nothing for it but to hearten her.

"Oh, but I can't! I'm much more likely to do him harm. You see I'm always forgetting."

"Forgetting what?"

"That I have the practice to take care of. I leave it at home, with my purse or my card-case, instead of carrying it about with me, wrapped in cotton-wool."

"Don't make the mistake of fancying Archie would like you to feel you ought to mix yourself up with his work. I'm sure he'd rather you left all that at home, as you say."

"Oh, but you don't understand! I keep thinking of myself as Patricia Sutherland—a young person who is free to go about the world and make such observations and criticisms as she pleases; whereas I ought always to be saying to myself, 'You are Mrs. Dr. Sutherland, and if you smile in the wrong place, you'll perhaps offend a patient.'"

"Patients are not so thin-skinned. They know when they've got hold of a good doctor, who understands their symptoms. That's the phrase, I believe."

"They certainly don't understand *my* symptoms," she laughed. "I'm always running my head against native prejudices, or shocking the local sense of humour. If I say anything funny they all stare—as if my poor little jokes were labelled, 'made in England'—and despise accordingly."

"To be honest, we don't think very highly of the brand."

"Oh, I know, no good thing comes out of any country but your own."

"Well, that's a fine healthy, patriotic sentiment."

"And so pleasant and nice for anybody who chances to have been born on the other side of Tweed!"

"My dear," said the schoolmaster, putting on his lecturing cap, "this country is yours now by adoption, and you'll do well to think the best you can of it. It's kindlier than you would suppose. We don't wear our hearts upon our sleeves; but that's not to say we're heartless, or that we've got nothing to say because we say little and say it ill. Caution is in our blood, and I don't know but what our friendship's worth more because it isn't just a thing to be picked up with the first handshake. Wait a little, and you'll judge Shawbridge more tenderly."

"But think of years of it—years upon years of it! Every woman that has any sort of excuse has called on me, and I've called on her; in a week or two she'll swoop down upon me again, and we'll say the same things, and sit in the same chairs, and drink out of the same tea-cups, and it will be all deadly, deadly dull!"

She dropped her work in her lap, and clasped her hands behind the knot of her red-brown hair, and looked out between the window-bars, as if she saw that coming greyness pictured on the sky.

"Is human nature such a different mixture in London, then?"

"In London? One is such a speck, such an atom there that one doesn't get frightened at one's own shadow. It has no room to lengthen out. There's no oppression in the routine of life if you don't hear the wheels go round; but here—here, I think I could get to listen to my heartbeats."

"Then you would be doing a very foolish thing."

"I know, I know;" she relaxed her arms and smiled. "You'll tell me I ought rather to model myself upon the Shawbridge house-wife. She's excellent of course: I dare say she quite comes up to your ideal of the truly feminine."

"And what may my ideal of the truly feminine be in your eyes?"

"Oh, a creature with what is called home accomplishments and no opinions. How many times have I been asked if I've made my jam yet! It doesn't interest me to talk of jam, or to be offered recipes. I'd rather talk of the new woman—at least she isn't insipid, like strawberry jam! Why should virtue always be so uninteresting? Oh, these women, they radiate the common place! The kitchen and the store-cupboard, the children's complaints, and the maids' carryings-on. Me! what a muddy, dull backwater they make of life! And there's the whole big sea to explore!"

"Oh, indeed! How very severe we are pleased to be. And is there so vast a difference, then, between the ordering of the pantry and the drawing-room? How can a lofty soul like yours unbend to the arrangement of a drapery, or the colour of the carpet?"

"That's different. A woman's drawing-room ought to be some sort of guide to her mind and tastes; but how can her jam pots be? One kind of jam pot is just like another —only more so."

"Well, and aren't the Shawbridge drawing-rooms, by your own allowing, an index to character? There's variety enough in them, as far as I've seen."

"Degrees of splendour. You've got to go one better than your neighbour, that's all. No; if one of these excellent housewives would have her jam pots made square, there would be some hope of her. There's salvation in original ideas; but as for her chairs—she's only got to have a brighter shade of satin and a little more gilding than they have next door, and her business is done."

The eternal feminine—how magnificently it sweeps over inconsistencies! Here was the same little lady who, a day or two before, had defended her choice of a library on the score of outward comeliness; her books were to applaud the binder's taste, and supplement the wall paper! But these little ebullitions of discontent were nothing but the froth coming uppermost at the bidding of a passing mood, and were no indication of storm. The deep places of her nature were yet to be stirred.

She missed Nancy, and sometimes railed at her in notes that ran after each other like rain-drops, and sometimes would be a whole week quite content and rather pleased to be left to her own devices.

"Will you go and see Mr. Cunningham when I'm gone?" Nancy had asked of her. "He will miss me less if you go," she said very simply.

Patricia promised. But why need Nancy go at all, and make Shawbridge unbearable for two people? Was life viewed from a "common stair"—a crowded "land" of un-gentle, busy folk, and many children, and noise of coming and going, overhead and underfoot, so desirable an exchange?

"Don't you hate poor relations?" said Patricia. "I know I should—only *we* were the poor relations of our family, you see."

"She's a cousin," said Nancy, with shocked

reproof, as if the tie made the cross old woman to whom she was going, almost sacred.

To Patricia it was an incomprehensible thing, this tenacious clinging to kinship which is so essentially Scotch; the enshrining of one's forebears is a part of religion with us, an ancestral practice that comes down from generation to generation, and is slow to die. It was excuse enough that Auntie Pringle had sent for her, but the occasion served Nancy doubly, though her honesty stopped short at confessing this to her friend. It was with a passionate hope that her father would miss her —if it were only at the hour for some little indulgence—that Nancy packed her trunk and went away. The nearness of their every-day life was getting to be sore; perhaps absence might heal it.

Patricia was slow to fulfil her promise. She had the shrinking of the young and the strong from anything in the shape of defeat, and the blind minister was a beaten man. To fail is so intolerable to youth, and half its pity is anger at fate.

Thus the days slipped away, and so it chanced that she never came face to face with the minister at all until her own trouble unlocked the door to his. By that gate alone we have the freedom of another's heart.

She was bound on some longer road one day, and the little victoria Sutherland had bought for her use was at the door. As she came out of the house—I with her, as was my practice, to see her off—and stood on the topmost step, a patient emerged from the side entrance, dismissed unhealed, poor soul, and hirpling away between two sticks.

Her eyes darkened as she followed his slow progress ; there was a touch of resentment in them, too. She only thought of Archie's practice in those days as a disturbing something that came between her and the perfection of her life ; it claimed him, his time, his tenderness, and she coveted every minute of him herself. But her face glowed and cleared as his firm step sounded across the hall.

"Where are you off to ? " he asked, a hand on her shoulder.

"Black Hall. Won't you come?"

He was running a critical eye over the chestnut, and the smart little carriage, and he said heedlessly, not noticing the appeal in her voice—

"You'll enjoy the drive. It's a glorious day."

"As if I wanted to go!" she said disdainfully. "I only go because I must. It's a horrid duty—like your medicine—nasty, and sure to disagree."

He laughed.

"You don't know much about my medicines," he said ; and indeed she looked her very best. Perhaps she had used some extra care in her toilet ; her dress was more filmy, with dropping laces, than usual, and feathers curled over the brim of her shady hat. He looked at her with honest admiration, but too much as if she were a pretty possession to be taken care of. Clever man as he was, he made the mistake of forgetting that every human being has a serious side, which can't afford to go undeveloped.

"If you would only take a holiday some-times," she said; but she turned her head aside, and again he missed the wistfulness.

"And what could happen to my work if I played tricks with it like that?" he asked, as he handed her into the carriage, and tucked the light summer rug about her knees.

"A career may cost too much, if it absorbs everything," she retorted.

To him it only seemed one of the sharp, half-stilted speeches she sometimes made, the quaint turn of a clever child; but to my ear there was an ominous truth in it. She was wondering, poor child, if he had forgotten that next day but one was her birthday. But he had not forgotten; his present was lying hidden away, ready for her; he had a punctilious memory for such little matters.

He looked at her pouting face teasingly for a moment. Then he said, as if it were a mere by the way—

"Suppose 1 could take a day off on Thursday?"

Her face was on an instant like sunshine.

"Oh, Archie, you will—you will!" She clutched his hand.

"If nobody chances to be dying for want of me."

"Oh, nobody could be so inconsiderate—on my birthday!"

"Well, then, goosie, and what will you do with me? Take me to make calls, I suppose? Mrs. Sutherland and her husband going out to tea!"

"Calls indeed!" she was all child again. "We'll stay at home, and see nobody. And if you're both very good I'll make you some almond toffee, and Friend Fowler will relate his love-affairs."

Sparkling, smiling, and triumphant, she went on her way, with a pretty dash and air that would presently make all Hill Street turn its head and crane its neck out of shop doors. Indeed, the dust of her progress made a little cloud that half obscured a Bath-chair, slowly pulled round the end of South Place by the perspiring and much-afflicted Andra Souttar. The occupant of it had a pair of beady-black eyes that saw most things, spectacles or none, and they embraced in one malignant sweep our two selves, still lingering on the door-step, and the little equipage and its smiling occupant.

"What's up with the old witch?" Sutherland asked, half surprised. "Looks as if one or other of us was in her black books."

"Oh, I'm the culprit, no doubt," said I, complacently enough; for, like a fool, I thought all was well since I had compelled her to silence about that matter of Cunningham and Sophia Green, and held her threats of vengeance in light enough esteem.

"By the way," he said, as he turned back to the surgery, "I haven't heard of her calling on Patricia."

"She hasn't called."

"And as well too. It's a face that would sour milk. But it's odd. I'd have thought curiosity would have brought her, if nothing else did."

"The fact is," said I, thinking it as well to get the affair over, "she came the day before

.you and Patricia returned, and I had occasion to snub her."

"Really!" he said, his eyes full of the kindliest laughter; "you're getting on, Harry, old man! So you've managed to make her afraid of you!"

"Yes," I repeated, ass that I was, "I've managed to make her afraid of me!"

CHAPTER IV.

HAD fallen in these days from the place I had held in Dr. Gillespie's esteem, and he let me know it, in his own inimitable way. Not that he ever let himself go, in a fine, natural burst of wounded resentment, as on that day in his study; he had put on his "Christian minister" manner once more, and perhaps I had never guessed the enormity of my offence save for the magnanimity of his forgiveness.

We met sometimes in the fieldpath, when I was on my way to the other Manse, and the man's art was a thing to wonder at. Without a word of reproach, his air, the quality of his handshake, the subdued resignation of his expression said plainer than speech—

" You have wounded me ; but, you see, I turn to you the other cheek."

He took Nancy's departure on a visit to Edinburgh as a grievance. He was not a man who cared to dip deeper than the surface of his own nature, but it went against his conceptions of a father's part to feel satisfaction in his only child's absence, and to excuse it he fostered his sense of affront. It let him slip, without a reminding prick of conscience, into fresh indulgences ; an extra glass or two of port at night when there was no one to talk to ; an extra hour or two of lie-a-bed in the morning to sleep off the bemusing effects. What was the use of rising when there was no one to keep waiting behind the tea-urn—no one with whom to discuss the day's news ? A house where there are only the women in the kitchen has little of the sense of home ; he had been widowed so long that now that Nancy had forsaken him, a relapse into bachelor ways was inevitable. He said it by way of reproach against her, but with an inward, shamed, uneasy joy at the larger liberty it gave him to play a grosser part.

In his soiled dressing-gown of a morning, unshaven, heavy-eyed, his mind put on the sloven too; his parishioners were little in the way of expecting spiritual counsel from him— he was not finished hypocrite enough for that —but if one chanced to call on him in the hours before the midday meal, the servant lass had orders to say he was not to be disturbed. To the unstudious there is no such temptation to idleness as a study. It is a seclusion all the world respects; for what should a man be busy with there if not the society of his books?

Bright little Sarah, who meant to take such good care of her minister in Miss Nancy's absence, had a scared look on her innocent face sometimes.

"I canna think what's come ower the maister," she said to Mrs. Ann Rutherford, the housekeeper. "He glowers at me whiles, as if he had gaen gyte."

"Tut; the man's busy," retorted Ann, who was long in the Manse's service, and who had that passionate pride in maintaining the house's honour that is a splendid virtue in an old servant. "Would ye hae him wasting his time on the likes of you? Set ye up! Awa', lass, to your work, an' dinna stand havering there."

But it was she who faced the visitors, after that, when they came at inconvenient hours, a thin, whipping-post of a figure, and it was she who slipped into the study in the early light of day, hiding the traces of last night's supper before the lass was allowed to enter with her dustpan and broom.

Once she had near shut me out on the door-step, with a slam of the door in my face, but relented and melted into a kind of civility when she knew I had only come to hand in a book.

"Ye'll be hearing from Miss Nancy, sir?" she asked when my message was delivered, and she had promised attention to it.

"Yes, she has written once or twice."

"She'll be biding in the town a whilie yet?"

"I fancy her cousin isn't very willing to spare her. Is there anything to bring her back specially ? There's nothing wrong ? " I asked, something in her face prompting the question.

" Wrang ! What suld gang wrang ? " she demanded, facing me with a dauntless grey eye. " I hae lookit efter this hoose, and the minister and Miss Nancy, and the hail hypothec these twunty year an' mair, sin the mistress slippit awa', an' I'm no' that failed yet, that I ken o', to be chairged wi' the neglect o' ma duty."

She whipped up her anger against me, to divert my supposed suspicions ; but indeed I had no fancy to come prying.

In the afternoon the minister would clothe himself anew in mind and body, when he set out on his visitations. These became more and more necessary to him, as his sense of injury grew with the brooding on it.

In the outset he had no thought to be disloyal to his child. It was the weakness of caring to be thought right ; it was the flatness of an afternoon mood wanting a fillip of some sort that drew him into it. A look, a sigh, a murmured word, was almost enough, and bit by bit the story grew till it would have shocked him to see in what fast, bold colours it was painted on his people's minds. At last Shawbridge saw the blind minister's adopted son for what it was now convinced he was— a profligate, a ne'er-do-well, a something worse than a drinker. For a love of honest toddy there may be found excuse, but the victim of the morphia habit stands in surer condemnation because his is a temptation impossible for the common mind to grasp. And the sins that are not our sins are ever the blackest.

And for this sorry lover Nancy was disobeying, defying, wounding to death the best and tenderest of fathers.

It was a fell injury for a father to do his child. A little earlier, and the man's pride would have withheld him from exposing the wounds of his own household ; but the better part of him had deteriorated under disappointment, and his hurt self-love was soothed by the ointment of his people's sympathy. If it seems a slap to their shrewdness that they believed him, remember the pedestal on which the minister stands in his own Scotch parish, the sacredness of his office, and, in this special case, the ornamentalness of the man, and the graciousness of his manner, that had long ago made Shawbridge too uplifted to ask what kind of qualities lurked beneath.

At the tea-hour he would still go to Mrs. Laidlaw's, and there, be sure, though the woman kept her bargain with me, his better impules got no wings.

Patricia and I were together one afternoon in Shaw Street, when we saw him coming to meet us.

Charlie Nairn was at her other side, for Charlie, with a boy's fervour, was a worshipper of young Mrs. Sutherland; but at sight of that imposing figure he slipped down Gibbs' Entry with the agility of an eel.

Patricia laughed.

" If I wasn't a staid matron," she remarked, " I would run after Charlie."

" Why ? " I asked. But there was no time

to hear her reasons before the big man was shaking hands with us both; he offered me his finger-tips, but he has a kindliness for a pretty woman, and presented Patricia with his whole palm.

"May I hope," he said, "that your destination is the same as mine?"

"I think that can scarcely be," said Patricia, demurely, "since we come from opposite poles."

"But we meet at Mrs. Laidlaw's doorstep."

"Indeed?" said Patricia, looking up at the green-painted door as if she had never seen it before. "Is this Mrs. Laidlaw's house? I think I have heard of her."

"You put it humorously," he said, and smiled as if she meant a jest, though he looked puzzled. "It would be difficult, even for Mrs. Sutherland, whose will must be law to all who know her, to live in Shawbridge without hearing of Mrs. Laidlaw."

"But," she answered softly, "to have heard of her would scarcely justify me in going uninvited to her 'at home,' would it? I'm afraid we must say good-bye, Dr. Gillespie. I hope you will have a very nice tea."

"But, my dear young lady——"

"We really mustn't keep you. I'm almost afraid there is some one watching for you at the window. It is a pity, for I should have liked to hear the very latest about Nancy."

His face stiffened.

"Your news is probably more recent than mine," he said, trying to carry the matter off easily. "We poor parents don't get much attention nowadays—a letter once a week or so, just to keep poor papa in a good humour. Now I dare say you hear every day?" His look had a kind of veiled anxiety in it.

"Not so often as that," said Patricia. "Dr. Gillespie, isn't it time Nancy came home?"

"If you can persuade her of that," he said, with his large graciousness well in hand once more, "you will be doing her old father a good turn. The Manse is very desolate without her."

"He doesn't want her to come back," said

Patricia, as we went upon our way. "Nancy's old father is like a little naughty boy—up to some mischief when his nurse's back is turned. And a nice playmate he has chosen!"

"Why, Patricia," I said, surprised at the intensity of her tone, "you've never met the redoubtable Mrs. Laidlaw!"

"But I call you to witness I've had a chance. Are you surprised at my strength of mind in refusing it?" she said.

"I'm flattered that you prefer my company."

"I can have your company any day, Friend."

"Then why didn't you accept the doctor's invitation? He would have been delighted to introduce you."

"If I had gone in, would you have gone also?"

"No."

"Very well, then, I had the same motive as you for staying outside."

"But I didn't give you my reasons."

"And I won't give you mine! But you

can take it for granted, if you like, that they are the same as yours. There's that miserable Charlie boy. Come here, sir, and account for your extraordinary behaviour."

"I remembered a sudden engagement," said the brazen Charles.

"The adult human is the natural foe of the boy," said I. "That's why Charlie prefers your company to the minister's."

"Thank you," she said majestically; "but I think I am quite old enough to take care of Charlie's morals. Come, confess what made you run away, unless it were a guilty conscience? What have you been up to, Charlie?"

"Nothin'. He isn't friendly to my personal interests." Then, abandoning his unaccustomed stilts, "He puts my back up, he does. He's a regular sneak. He would think nothin' of rounding on me to the old woman."

"I suppose that means that you are playing truant. If Mr. Fowler and I did our duty by you, we ought to march you back to the mill as our prisoner of war. But old people should remember that they were young once."

She looked at me severely.

"That shouldn't be awfully hard for you to do, you know," said Charlie, cheerfully, leaving his fate in her hands.

"Well, of course I haven't quite so far to grope back as Mr. Fowler; but I do seem dimly to remember that it was rather nice to be naughty when you weren't found out. If I were to ask you to tea now, by way of punishment — to tea and raspberries and cream. You can eat raspberries, I suppose, being such a very human boy? Well, then, if I were to be so very kind to you, you would be contrite, wouldn't you, and would promise never to be so wicked again as to evade your parish priest?"

"Never," said Charlie, fervently, "until the next time!"

Charlie had already at four of the clock, scarce an hour previously, laid in a substantial stock of provender; but where is the boy who cannot triumph over any number of miscellaneous meals? So we bought the rasp-berries, the birds being free to such as grew in our own small patch, and carried them to the shadow of the weeping ash, where Sutherland, coming home in a hurry between two cases, found us, and was tempted to linger for a few minutes.

"I say, Dr. Sutherland," said the terrible boy, his mouth full, "you tell Mrs. Sutherland the minister's an old humbug. She won't believe *me*."

"Then I should despair of convincing her," said Sutherland, laughing.

"The father of Nancy is sacred," said Patricia, with gay authority. "I forbid you all to discuss him. Nobody could help being good who belonged to Nancy. You think her perfect, don't you, Archie?"

"I think you a very loyal friend," he said gently.

*　　*　　*　　*　　*

There was one other in whose thoughts the father of Nancy must not be allowed to step down from his pedestal. Late that night, Ann Rutherford slipped from her bed, on which the moonlight shone, making a cold, pure radiance about her troubled face. Her long, thick black hair—her woman's one glory—hung in a heavy wave down her white bed-gown. She thrust it impatiently from her forehead, but did not stop to coil it, though she huddled on a skirt, and sat on the edge of the mattress to draw the ribbed grey woollen hose over her bare feet. A moment she paused—listening sternly for the girl's regular breath—by the bed near the door where Sarah slept.

"She's fast," said Ann to herself, and, indeed, the girl was smiling, as if that silver splendour were inwoven in her dreams. No fear that she would waken at anything so soundless as the slip-slipping of Ann's stockinged feet down the wooden stair and across the narrow hall, that she should start up or creep to the stairhead, dumfounded to see Ann—the righteous, stern Ann—stoop, with an ear at the study door, in the wee small hours of the night, when all honest folk were abed, and listen guiltily there, as if to steal the master's secrets.

Ann clutched her bedgown over the place where her heart was making such a riot that its thumps were like the fall of a sledge-hammer in her ears.

"The Lord grant I am wranging the man," she said; but in a minute more, controlling herself by a strong effort, she heard the tinkle of clinking glass, as if a decanter were held by an unsteady hand.

Her purpose came to her then. She glanced at the long clock, and saw by the moonlight on the dial that the hand pointed almost to two. She drew herself up—she was a tall woman—to her full height, and opening the study door, went quietly in.

"Maister," she said, the respectful servant still, anxious to shield him even from himself, "I'm thinking ye'll hae been takin' a bit nap, or maybe your watch is run down; ye'll no' be aware that it's chappet twa frae the Free Kirk steeple; an' though I'm no' sayin' yon auld Dissentin' knock is a gude time-keeper——"

She broke down there at sight of the besotted face he lifted to her.

"Minister!" she cried, her voice lifted and strenuous to reach his dulled ears, and yet with what an undertone of sorrow and shame and grief in it. "Come awa' to your bed, come awa', and there's naebody but Ann—that has served ye half her life-time—will ever ken onything. Would ye be fand here, wi' the wine red in the cup afore ye, when the lass comes ben in the mornin' to dicht an' soop the room—you a minister o' the Gospel, an' the best respecket in a' Shawbridge?"

Though she spoke with a mixture of chiding and remonstrance—as a mother who scolds and forgives in a breath—there was the keenest dread in the glance of her grey eyes. He was big and buirdly, in the very prime of his strength—if he chose to defy her—in madness to thrust her from the room, maybe, or to sit on there, sodden and helpless, dozing into forgetfulness till daylight found him out and she could no more hide the black shame and affront of his condition from other eyes—what could she do? She was but a woman, when all was told, and no match for him, if he were minded to resist her pleading.

But he had not yet reached the quarrelsome stage of intoxication, and when he stuttered thickly and disjointedly, with maudlin dignity, that Ann was mistaken—he was ill—any one could see that he was ill—an illused man —forsaken by his child—a little wine—for the stomach's sake—Apostolic injunction— she drew a smothered breath of relief, while she said, with what cheerfulness she could assume—

"Ay, it's easy seein' ye're no weel. Ye look rael weary-like, an' it's late—late. It's an airm up the stair ye'll be wantin', an' I'm just fair gled I thocht to look in, seein' the spunk o' licht still shining through the sneck. Ye'll be better atween the sheets, minister, an' ye'll just sleep fine an' cosy, an' wauken wi' no' sae muckle as a sair heid the morn."

With infinite pains and patience she coaxed

him to rise from his chair and cross the room, and helped his unsteady progress up the creaking stair, his heavy foot stumbling at every second step, so that her heart was in her mouth lest the lass's sound sleep should be broken at last, and she come out wondering and frightened to spoil all.

But she got him to his room and to bed at last, where he wept upon his pillow in inarticulate. self-pity, and in the middle of those insensate tears—every drop fell on her heart like a flake of fire—fell snoringly asleep.

Not thus had he wept, not thus had she mourned, when the young mistress died, and she, but new in his service, had not dared to comfort him.

She happed the clothes about him with a careful hand, and stood looking down on him with a face that was wan and grey in the cold searching light; it was a moment when, herself unseen, she dared let emotion loose, and face the vision of her fallen pride.

Then she turned away, and tidied the

disarray of the room with methodical patience, folding his garments neatly on a chair, and setting the water-bottle and tumbler on a little table within his reach. On another night she would have left the Bible there too, where for years on years she had placed it at nightfall with the candle and the matches. The book had been his mother's, it had a purple binding and big silver clasps, and there was a faded ribbon between the leaves at the place in the Gospels where she had read her last chapter. But on this night Ann lifted the book and put it back on the chest of drawers.

"Ye're no' fit for it yet," she said sadly, speaking in to herself; "an' I daur'na dishonour the word o' God."

The house was still, wrapped in silence, when she crept downstairs again, to air the room, heavy with the sickly scent of wine, and put away the decanters in the sideboard. A glass had been broken, and some of the contents had escaped over his scattered papers. Ann held her candle close, and saw that the stained pages belonged to the famous old sermon upon the prodigal son, over which so many had wept, and he with them.

" Ye'll no' preach that again—no' for ithers—for a whilie," she said, and with a stern hand collected the manuscript, and laying it on the hearth, struck a match and set it alight. The wine-stain burned slow, and her pride in him—the gallant handsome man, minister and master in one—burned with it. It was as if he had set his seal on this written page from which he had preached no later than Sunday gone by, aiming, as everybody knew, at Frank Cunningham, to show that he, too, had gone journeying down that broad road to the Far Country.

Ann sat a long time by the open window, the cool air clearing her hot brain, and steadying her faithful heart to the task it had set itself.

Nobody must know—she would be bathed in shame as the garden was drenched in moonlight if so much as a whisper went forth of that which her eyes had seen.

"Miss Nancy maun come hame," she said, "he'll no' daur, wi' the lassie lying waukrife in the room aboon him. He's been ower lanesome; ay, that's it, he's no' the kind that can be left his lane, without seekin' to hearten himself wi' unlawful means. But what excuse to gie the lassie—me that has aye fleeched at her to bide awa' when ance she has set out, an' tak' her fill o' the town pleasures? It beats me what kind o' lee 'll serve ma turn best, an' no' gie her a glimmer o' the truth, puir bairn. Ay," she said at last, after a long pause, as a solution of the difficulty came to her, "that 'll e'en hae tae dae: I canna mak' a better o' 't."

CHAPTER V.

"IT is borne in upon me that I shall be reluctantly compelled to refuse," said Patricia; we three were seated at breakfast, and the day's post was under discussion. It brought among other things a belated dinner invitation to the Castle. "I know there's an excellent reason tucked away somewhere, if I could only lay hands on it."

"Produce it, then," said Sutherland, "and I'm your man. But mind it's a genuine one."

"Dear me, if we were going anywhere else, we should have to adhere to the strictest letter of the truth, or be made to suffer for it; but the Castle people—Lady Minterley is a woman of the world, and she'll only say,

'Those Sutherlands can't come; well, we've done the civil thing by them. We must fill up their places. Whom shall we ask?' Besides, I remember now why I can't go. Do you know how long we've been married, Archie? There," she turned to me tragically, "I knew he couldn't tell. Isn't it a fine compliment that he can't remember his own wedding-day!"

"Give me a minute and I'll make the calculation. Let me see, it was June, the week old Mrs. Baird died."

"That's the way he chronicles his domestic joys," she said ironically. "The week so-and-so had the measles; the day such-and-such a baby was born! Well, it was June, as it happens, and this is September, and how often do you suppose I've worn my wedding finery in the interval?"

"We have eaten a good many dinners at other folks' expense."

"My frock could tell that tale! It's impossible; only fit to be put aside as a relic for my grandchildren to play charades in. You wouldn't like me to go to the Castle with a soiled hem, would you, dear ? "

" A soiled what ? " Sutherland asked, in a preoccupied voice, busy shaving the thinnest slices from the ham.

" Hem, my dear sir, hem. I'm as draggle-tailed as the eagles at the Zoo."

" Well, you can put on fresh plumage, like them, can't you ? " he said lightly.

" I'm afraid not. They only get new uniforms once a year, poor beasties, and I'm expected to advertise my happiness by wear-ing my wedding livery for at least six months."

" Then you'll have to buy a new hem, I suppose," he said, with masculine vagueness.

" Listen to him, listen to the man ! " She derisively addressed the ceiling. " He says I can buy a new hem, and he has been married four months ! "

" I've been a very backward pupil," he said, laughing ; " but that's because I haven't had the privilege of paying the dressmaker's bill yet. Seriously, Patricia, I'm afraid we'll have to go. Lord Minterley has been very civil, and we've no engagement."

"Oh, I know, the practice!" she said resignedly. "Dear, do you know, I sometimes wish you were a quack."

"Heavens!" cried Sutherland, letting fall knife and fork; "what an ambition."

"We could advertise openly then. You could even sell your syrups and your pills from a nice little covered cart, and offend nobody. Oh, wouldn't it be fun! I would come and help you with my persuasive tongue, and you could show me off as a convincing proof of their virtues. I know my nose isn't immaculate, but I have rather a nice complexion."

"What a heap of nonsense the baby talks!" said Sutherland, a trifle ruffled perhaps, but holding himself in bravely.

"I don't think it's so very nonsensical," she said wilfully. "Is it any wiser to dress up, and eat dinners you don't want to eat, just to keep people in a good humour? Every time I put on my satin and pearls, I feel as if I had a paper pinned to my back. 'I'm Mrs.

Dr. Sutherland, and I'm here to show myself off, and to prove to you he's really respectably married; and please, I'm on my very best behaviour, and will try not to offend you. And will you kindly call in my husband next time you're ill?' It would be ever so much simpler and—and honester too, to sell the bread pills openly, at a shilling and a penny halfpenny a box."

Sutherland coloured, and for a moment his forehead contracted, but he had infinite patience with her when she was in her wayward moods, and he only said gently—

"I think I wouldn't say that, if I were you."

She looked at him, and when she saw that she had displeased him, the petulance died out of her face. To have offended him would have been the eclipsing of her sun at noontide; and he never guessed, or came near guessing, how she loved the very ground he trod on.

She rose, and went to him and knelt by him. Neither of them minded the third person who was present.

"Archie dear," she said, with a tender kind of dignity that seemed to me moving, "I haven't said anything really naughty, have I? You know my silly tongue runs away with me; but I don't mean any harm, and I wouldn't say things like that to anybody else except you, and Friend here, for the world. It's just because—because it's so much cosier to dine at home, just we three together."

"Of course it is, goosie," he said, lifting her chin with one hand and looking at her quizzingly, his momentary irritation subdued. "But in the grown-up world you've got to do some things you don't like with the best grace you can. We are all servants of the public, whatever our trade, and it's our business to please it without cringing or stooping. There's nothing very honourable, that I know of, in being rude and disobliging, though some people seem to think you can't be moral unless you are. And does it never occur to you that I want to show off my wife, and have all the world admire her?"

Why didn't he add, "As I do?" Did she

miss that touch that would have been more to her than all the rest?

She looked at him with a world of wistfulness in her clear eyes.

"Sometimes," she said slowly, "sometimes I think you've married the wrong sort of woman. You should have had some one splendid and brave and serene, like Nancy. She couldn't be small-minded."

He turned very pale, but he never took his eyes from her face; it seemed to me she must hear the hoarseness in his voice, betraying the effort with which he said playfully—

"But I am Patricia's husband, you see."

Her love was her armour; her confidence lay sure behind it.

"Yes," she said gaily, "and you've got to make the best of this piece of imperfection! Well, I'll furbish up my gown with a new hem, and I dare say it'll pass muster, and I'll write and say we accept the Castle invitation, and Friend Fowler shall have his favourite dishes to make up for our absence. It's very mean of them not to ask him too, isn't it? He's a member of the firm!"

She came to me later in the morning, and sat on what she called the stool of repentance. She had a sock of Archie's in her hand which she darned fitfully — sign thrown out of her wifely allegiance. There was so much of the girl playing a pretty part, and loving it because it was pretty, in her still, and so soon there was to be no more.

"I'm afraid I was cross with Archie this morning," she said, "and irreverent towards the Practice. I'm going to bestow a big P on it after this, and put it in a glass case as an object of 'virtue and bigotry.' You know, Friend, my father was a soldier. He was a very young one, quite a boy-soldier —that's why we were so poor—when he died, and I think he must have bequeathed his fighting instincts to me, just in the crude, fermenting stage in which he left them. He had no chance to distinguish himself in a real, 'bluggy' battle, so he had to let fly at the windmills that came in his way. Mamma says he had a very irritable, undomestic kind of temper, but I don't think for a moment it is true. Anybody who married Lord Mortlake, who hasn't the spirit of a mouse, might think him cross, perhaps, but who wants a man to be a nincompoop? (You wouldn't believe Lord Mortlake was a really courageous soldier, would you? But he was, and papa's friend as well.) Well, where was I? Oh, about the windmills! The Practice is my windmill; I'm always wanting to run papa's sword at it. It is such a nuisance; it interferes with all my pleasures, and one has got to be so polite to it; and so careful not to tread on its old toes. Oh, I forgot," she clapped her hand to her mouth. "I said I was going to be respectful after this! Friend, do you think Archie really minds the rubbish I talk?"

"Not so long as he recognizes it for rubbish —it's your own word; but possibly he might prefer it if you took his work a little seriously."

"Really? But if we were both serious, wouldn't it be a little doleful? We'll have time to pull long faces!"

"It's his life's business — his deliberate

choice, and his whole heart is in it.   Hasn't he a right to ask that you should respect his work ? Besides, there's a splendid side to the profession, if you could only see it."

"But I married Archie—the man, not Dr. Sutherland, the physician and surgeon."

"You can't separate them, it would be wiser not to try.   A man's work is, or ought to be, a bit of himself."

"That doesn't seem to leave much room for the wife," she said, a little forlornly.   "It's the mistake we make, we girls, in thinking that we are really going to be our husband's other halves.   Somebody should tell us that that is only a polite form of speech, and that if we're allowed to occupy a poor quarter of their thoughts we ought to feel very truly grateful.   Every single patient Archie has, has a better claim on his time and his thoughts than I."

"Bless you, child, do you suppose if he were a lawyer it would be any different—or an author—wouldn't he put his clients, or his editor, or his publisher, in the front rank too, in

working hours, unless he were a fool ?   If you
had wanted a man to sit all day on the other
side of the fire, and discuss frocks and ribbons,
and the tittle-tattle of kitchen and drawing-
room, you should have married some fool of
quality, with inherited money enough to be
idle on, and too few brains to despise himself."

"As if I would change Archie for all the
world!" she said lightly, with a proud thrown-
back head. "I'd rather be his wife if he
blacked shoes in Shaw Street than call the
grandest peer husband. The truth is, Friend,
since I am doing penance, I will whisper to you
that I am jealous—jealous of wife No. 1, Mrs.
Practice ! She takes away that other quarter
of him that I thought I was marrying ; but, as
he chose her first, I suppose I must put up
with her, horrid old thing !"

" Make a friend of her, and you'll find she's
quite harmless."

She made a little grimace.

"Oh, as I told you," she said, " I'm going
to give her all her dues after this, and let

Archie worship her as much as he pleases. And besides, I'm not going to be lonely any more. (You know, Friend, though you are very nice, you're only a man after all.) I have a most lovely piece of news! Nancy is coming home! This very day!"

"That's sudden, isn't it? Ann Rutherford gave me no hint when I was at the Manse the other day."

"You call it sudden, and she's been gone two months! Much *you* miss her! Well, it's Ann who is bringing her home, Ann, and a delightful, mysterious person called the 'travelling merchant.' Do merchants never move from home in Scotland that he should be singled out for this distinction?"

"On the contrary, I fancy this manner of merchant employs his whole time in travel. But why should the packman bring Nancy home?"

"Why? Who cares? She's coming, and that's enough. I'll buy his whole pack myself, if he calls, out of gratitude to him for proving such a magnet."

This was the only device on which Ann had been able to hit. Old Adam Grindley had supplied the housewives of Shawbridge with linen from the Belfast looms in the days when shops were fewer, and the spring or autumn visits of the pedlar were an event to count on, and some old-fashioned people still preferred to supply their needs from the veteran's bale. He had had the Manse's patronage for two generations, and Ann wrote that she couldn't " even " herself to choose the new tablecloths. Perhaps Nancy was glad to catch at so flimsy an excuse to end a visit that had not fulfilled all she hoped from it ; at any rate, she was coming home.

"And I am going to run down to the Manse to leave a message for her. She is to arrive at three, and why shouldn't she come here for tea ? 'Poor papa' will have had two hours of her by that time, and he will want to go and see his Mrs. Laidlaw, and will be very much obliged to me for giving him an excuse. There's Archie "—she started up, her face all lit and smiling. " He must have forgotten something ; he said he wouldn't be home till dinner."

She flung the stocking from her unceremoniously, and in a moment was up and out of the room, leaving the door open behind her, and was skimming downstairs, calling his name as she went.

I heard him chide her as he caught her at the last step, and her gay laugh answering him.   How long was it before I heard her laugh like that again ?

*   *   *   *   *

She told me when we met at lunch that Sutherland would be late, and that we were to dine without him.

" Perhaps we can coax Nancy to stay," she said.   " You do like her, don't you, Friend ? "

" Yes," I said, " I like her."   And she was quite content.

I stood at the door a minute, watching her, the lace of her parasol rising and falling in the pleasant wind.   It was a perfect day, the first of St. Martin's little summer.   The gentle saint can claim but a brief three days, in our northern latitudes, and then scowling storms are on his track. Patricia turned at the corner, and waved to me.

When she had left her message at the Manse, and was turning homewards again, an idle impulse led her into the churchyard. The trees, still full and green, had an invitation, for the sun beat down with June's fervour. She had never strayed in here before, shunning it rather, with averted head; her youth had so little in common with this solemn resting-place of the dead, but to-day the exaltation of her mood lifted her above all morbid fears.

She thrilled at the exquisiteness of life—the world was beautiful, she scarce knew why, except that she was happy. The future beckoned with new wonders, strange joys. The little shudders that ran through her were not born of fear, but of pure content. She did not say to herself, " How proud I ought to be because Archie loves me—chose me." That would not have been natural. Love was a force that had swept them together; from all time it was decreed that they should meet, and love, and marry. Husband and wife—on that level they stood equals, each delighting to give his all.

"And some day I shall be the mother of his child," she said to herself. Her blushes were for the wonder, and the awe, and the goodness of it.

She wandered here and there among the careless stones, bending this way and that, as if they were weary of recording the virtues of the long-forgotten sleepers beneath, the moss of time obliterating their very names. A kind of pity that gave a quicker edge to her own joy, moved her for these lonely, forsaken folk. Could they feel the summer stir in their bones? Did memory somewhere survive of their loves and griefs and hopes? Oh, they had never loved and been loved as she! The life that beat and bounded in her pulses must outlive a hundred deaths, itself deathless.

She sat on a great flat stone, raised table-wise from the earth on four supports. In such-wise were graves guarded long ago, as if uneasy ghosts might walk, or the sun filter through the soil, or unbidden seedlings spring to make a green covering for the last sleep.

Patricia leaned a hand upon the sun-steeped stone, and tried to read the worn lettering. A husband had cut it there once to tell the world that he was widowed.

"Here lies all that was mortal——"

She could decipher no more. She gave a little triumphant laugh.

"But the immortal part—he couldn't stifle that with this great stone he laid on your chest. Who were you? What were you, woman without a name? Did your heart ever sing as mine is singing? And were you glad when he gave up the world too, and they put him under this stone beside you? If I go first, I shall waken from the soundest sleep when Archie comes back to me. I should know it if it were a thousand years!"

But the thought of that separation, that reuniting could not stay with her, took no hold of mind or fancy. Death came to others

—to those whose faded stories belonged to history; but life was hers, abounding life, rich with purpose and with promise.

She looked up into the tree-tops. A sapless leaf, first of autumn's harvest, fluttered down now and then, going to its own grave. She caught it idly with outstretched hands, and played with it. She leaned back, and looked up into the green roof above her, where the light wind soughed, and the trees were talking to each other in that shriller voice they learn with the waning year, like gossips grown old.

"They see something coming that we down here cannot see," she said to herself; then at the thought that she too had a secret, she thrilled again.

Should she tell Nancy, some day? Oh, not yet, but some far-off day, when it was less new, less sacred, and wonderful? A new and serious, a pensive gentleness came upon her face. "I must be very good," was her thought, "for the sake of this gift that is coming to me." And, somehow, goodness seemed easy, as natural as the happiness that bathed her.

What the tree-tops looked down upon was an old lady, walking slowly, on the arm of another and a smaller woman, down the broad central path, between the crowding obelisks and crosses. At Patricia's tombstone she halted; and the girl, coming swiftly down from the clouds, saw her vision fade, as if a mist rising from the earth had blotted it out. This old, ugly grinning woman was a bit of the common everyday world, where pretty fancies have no place.

"Nay, my dear, you'll not be running away from me as if we were strangers?" she was addressed, as she made a movement to rise. "I know you fine, you're the bonnie bride, young Mrs. Sutherland, that all Shawbridge is clean daft about. Maybe you've heard tell of me too, for I've reigned here longer than you."

"You are Mrs. Laidlaw, I think?" said Patricia, without warmth.

"Just the very same; Jennet Laidlaw, at

your service, an old failed woman. If you will make room for me, I'll rest awhile beside ye, and make your better acquaintance. Away with ye, McAlister, and dismiss Andra Soutar, or the body will be chairging me for his meditation among the tombs. Ye can take a turn among them yourself, for that'll no cost me a bawbee, and it'll be more profitable for you than standing here on your feet glowering at me, and pleasanter for me that has no mind ye should hear our cracks. Hoots, woman, what gars ye linger? Are ye feared ony hurt will come to me? Where could ye leave me in better company than with our young lady here?"

The day had lost its heaven-born look, it was of the earth earthy now. Patricia unwillingly made room for this disturber of her peace. She vaguely felt the hostility of the glance under the careful smile, and, scenting battle, had a mind to decline the encounter.

But pride forbade flight. "She shall not think she can frighten me," she said, and smiled the impulse away disdainfully.

Miss McAlister, who, greatly daring, had hovered lingeringly near, now drifted sadly down the walk, her round face screwed and contorted with childish distress.

CHAPTER VI.

"LET me go," said Nancy.

She lifted her hand, and in her voice there was authority, the kind of authority a woman wears when she thinks her province is about to be invaded, as from behind the closed door we heard the pitiful stifled sobbing.

"What have you done to her?" she asked, in a low voice of indignation, looking at me as if I ought to be ashamed of myself. "She was so happy!"

"God knows what has happened," I said, too distressed to be indignant at the implied accusation; "she came home like this a little while ago, and she will tell me nothing."

She put me gently aside—and indeed, what

place had I near a grief I could neither comprehend nor soothe?—and, going into the room, shut the door behind her.

"Dear," she said, "it is I, Nancy, come back to you."

Patricia, crouching in the big easy-chair—her trembling steps had carried her no further than the dining-room—quivered at the sound of the voice, but she did not move or speak. Her hat had fallen on the floor, her head was bowed upon her crossed arms, the fair proud head so lightly carried an hour or two before.

"What is it?" said Nancy, with tender persuasiveness, kneeling on the floor and gathering the shrinking girl in her strong arms with protective gentleness. "Tell Nancy what has grieved you. See, dear; I got your little note, and I came at once. I was so glad to come, it has been so lonely without you. Oh, you don't know how I've missed you, and how I said to myself in Edinburgh every morning, 'I'm one day nearer Patricia, my first and only girl friend;' and now you are in trouble, and you will not let me share it. Oh, don't break my heart with your silence, dearest; isn't it suffering for me to see you suffer?"

Patricia shuddered, and a low moan broke from her.

"No one can comfort me," she said.

"Then let me be sorry with you."

"You!" said Patricia, with a gasping cry. "You! Oh, Nancy, it is you whom I should hate and fear."

"Me?" said Nancy, wonderingly, with an inward spasm of dread, lest some sudden shock had turned the young thing's brain. "Why," she said, with assumed cheerfulness, "that would be silly indeed if you should begin to hate the friend who loves you so. And what is a friend for, but to carry half the trouble-burden? Even if I cannot help you, love, it will be easier for you if you will tell me what it is that is grieving you; things sometimes look less black when we see them through another person's eyes."

"My world can never be bright again;" the words had the accent of despair.

"Ah, don't say that; the worst has never happened to us when those we love are faithful still. Think of your husband."

"My husband!" she wailed. "I have no husband!"

Nancy was terribly perplexed. She knew, for I had told her so, that Sutherland had left home in his usual spirits, sped on his way by his wife, and that no whisper of any evil befalling him had reached the house. Patricia had only gone to the Manse—a mere ten minutes' walk; and in the word or two she had exchanged with Ann Rutherford at the door, the housekeeper had found her radiant.

"She's fair carried wi' delight at the thocht o' seeing ye, Miss Nancy," she had said. "My word, but it's graund to come hame to sic a welcome!"

And this was the welcome Nancy found waiting her. She went over every possible explanation in her anxious mind. There was no letter, no visitor to thrust the blame on. Patricia had gone out gaily, and when next she was seen she was stricken with seemingly inconsolable grief. Could this be the first sign of some physical or mental disturbance? Did—did madness lie that way?

Her heart gave sick leaps at the thought. But no, Patricia was too sound-natured, too well-balanced, to yield to a sudden fit of hysterics, or a morbid mood of home-sickness. Besides, was she not the happiest of happy wives? It had always given Nancy a whole-hearted content to think that here was one marriage that fulfilled one's dreams of what the tie should be. Oh for the husband's presence now! If he were but here, all would be well. She took no account of those frenzied words in which Patricia had cried out that she had no husband. It was but the fever in her veins. How hot her hands were, even through the gloves she still wore. Nancy busied herself gently with unbuttoning and pulling them off the unresisting fingers, all the while murmuring little soft words of love and sooth-ing. She longed to rise and slip from the room, and send a mounted messenger to inter-cept Sutherland and bring him home; but

Patricia's sobs were quieting a little, her head was dropped heavily on Nancy's shoulder, and she dared not move, dreading a return of the storm.

She was cramped and stiff with crouching; but she knelt on motionless, supporting the girl's weight, thankful that the shrinking resistance with which Patricia would at first have repulsed her had died away. And at last her infinite patience, and the magnetism of her love and sympathy, had their reward.

Patricia lifted a wan face out of which the mirth and life and delight in living had all died, and whispered—

"I ought to hate you, Nancy, but I can't. And oh," she moaned, "I don't wonder that he loves you best!"

Nancy felt a shock go through her strong frame, a great wave of fierce anger and indignation. The light was breaking on her now, and for a moment it seemed to blind her.

"Who told you that, told you a wicked lie!" she said, steadying her vibrating voice with a great effort.

"Oh no, no, no. It is true, and I was blind—a fool, not to know it."

"Hush, Patricia!" said Nancy, sternly. "You do not know what you are saying. You are disloyal to the husband whom you promised to honour. In marriage it is a crime to distrust."

"It is all so plain to me now," Patricia went on, unheeding; "and, you see, I am not angry. How can I be angry with you for being what you are? You are made for people to look up to and to love; and when they care for you they cannot stop caring, or be content with anything else. But I—I was so happy. She might have left me my poor little dream. What harm have I, a stranger, done her that she should pluck the heart out of my bosom to stab it? It would have hurt nobody—nobody, if I had been allowed to dream on; and now I shall have to live till I am old—old, and never another happy, careless day!"

"Who told you this?" Nancy asked, yet knowing the answer all the time.

"It was in the churchyard," Patricia sobbed on, in her weary, tired voice. "I had been to the Manse to leave the note for you, and then I went into the churchyard. I wanted to rest and think. I was so happy that it seemed as if even the dead people would be a little glad if they knew. I wanted to take my happiness out and look at it—it seemed so strange and wonderful; and yet as if I had a right to it too—as if God had meant it for me."

"So He did," said Nancy, with quiet conviction. "Hold to that, dear. God meant—He means your happy life to be yours, and nobody can take it away from you."

"Ah, but she has robbed me of it! How can it ever be the same again now that I know——"

"Patricia, listen to me," said Nancy. "No, wait; hear me first. I know who has done this wicked thing—who has tried to sow distrust in your mind, and I know why she has done it. It is to punish others—those who love you. Your husband, perhaps, if he has offended her, or your husband's friend—or—even me. And what she wanted most was to see that you believed her, because in that way she knew she would be stabbing those others who would rather, far rather, suffer themselves than that you should have a moment's pain. But, dear, it would have been better, braver, if you had refused to listen."

"I did—I did!" said Patricia, with revivifying indignation. "Do you suppose I was going to let her see that I cared—that I believed a word she said? But, oh, Nancy, it is true; and all the time she was speaking to me, though I defied her to her face, I knew it—in my heart."

"How can it be true," said Nancy, speaking with patient gravity, "when he has chosen you out of all the world? Are you not his wife? Do you forget all that that implies?"

"But he loved you first."

Patricia lifted her head and looked—her own tear-dimmed—in her friend's eyes; there was a longing wistfulness in her voice that seemed to say, "Deny it; tell me it is not so."

Nancy met the challenge steadily, though the colour burned in her cheeks like a fire.

"It is true that he thought he cared for me," she said; "but he was mistaken, and he found it out very soon. And, dear, he did you no dishonour, even when he made that mistake, for he did not know you—had not even seen you then. They told him he ought to marry; that, as a doctor, it would help him in his work, and it chanced that he saw more of me than of other girls here; but I—I had nothing to give him, nothing but the regard and respect I have for him still, as a good and honourable man."

Patricia's head had drooped again.

"You cared for Frank—always?"

"Always." The word had a world of truth and force in it.

"Tell me," Patricia whispered; "how was it? Did the love begin with you, or did he —was it he who spoke of it first?"

"I think there never was a time when we

did not care for each other," said Nancy, speaking cheerfully, leaping at the chance of diverting the other's thoughts; "and somehow it did not seem to need telling. He came here when he was very little, a little lonely boy, and shy and strange to the new world he found himself in; and I was a big girl and—and not shy," she laughed; "and it began with my taking care of him. We were playmates, and boy and girl together; and then, as we grew older, we seemed to change places—he was so much quicker, cleverer; he knew so much, much more. And the man should be the head of the woman; that is his right, and the happiest for both. She may still be first in all the little ways of caring and serving; but he goes out into the world, and experiences come to him that she, at home, can never know; and in the things that matter, it is for him to judge."

Patricia was listening, uncomforted. She had not failed because she had striven to be first. She had placed her husband on a pedestal, as a god to look up to, and she could never get near him, or reach him, or be anything to him, since she had never touched his heart. "If he had loved me, I could have helped him, even if I had been silly," was her confused thought. She moved her head wearily on Nancy's shoulder.

"And when he went to London you were engaged?" she asked.

"No, not then, though I think we both held ourselves pledged. It was later, when he had been gone a year or more, and was getting on, and making a name, and seeing the road open to the future"—her voice was studiously cheerful, though a quick ear might have caught an under-note of pain; for where was that bright future now? "It was then that he wrote."

"He wrote?"

"That he was working for me, seeing every day our life together coming nearer."

"He told you that—that he needed you—could not do without you—wanted your help?"

Nancy felt the convulsive pressure of Patricia's hand upon her arm, and was troubled ; but she answered lightly—

"What else is love between two people, but that they care supremely to be together, and miss something that is best in them when they are apart? Need you ask that, foolish child, you who know the answer so well ?"

"No," said Patricia, with a dull kind of despair ; "I know nothing. It is all a strange language to me. Archie was the first who came into my life to stir and change it, and I gave him everything, all my heart. But he did not say he could not do without me, not even that it would make his life happier if I shared it with him."

"Because he knew that you knew it. When people trust and understand each other, what is the use of so many words— as if they were strangers still ?"

"Hush !" the poor child put up a feverish hand, and laid it on Nancy's lips to silence her.

"Your story is not my story, and you only

wound me when you talk like that. I see it all now, as he must have seen it. I will tell it you, though it is my woman's shame. I was not very happy at home; you have no mother, and you would not understand how people may live together and do the same things and yet be miles apart. That was the way with mamma and me, and her marriage was only making things worse. So I was rebellious and unhappy, and one day when he—Archie—came and found me alone, and was kind and seemed sorry, I couldn't help crying. And he tried to comfort me, and—and somehow—I let him see—let him guess what I felt—and hoped—and wanted most in all the world. I was only a girl; I had never had a lover—not a real one, who spoke to me himself — and when he asked me to let him take care of me, I said yes, oh so joyfully; and when he kissed me and said he would try and make me happy, I thought—oh, the blind fool that I was !— that he had chosen me, too, and not just that he had pity on a wayward, discontented girl, because he is kind, and doesn't like to see anybody suffer. And I have been so happy in my fool's Paradise all this time!"

"You speak wildly; it is you, now, that are unreasonable and foolish," Nancy remonstrated, with a touch of sternness, forbidding herself to think for a moment that there might be even a shadow of truth in the broken confession. "Oh, think of it, Patricia, marriage is such a terrible thing, it draws people so close, and just because it is irrevocable—like dying, a wound once given is so ill to mend. It binds people so that they cannot escape; they must go on side by side, and the sore frets, because neither can leave the other and be alone to let it heal. And that is what happens when we who love lose faith in each other. To distrust poisons all life. There is no happiness for us any more. Love which was Heaven becomes Hell. You dishonour your husband when you doubt him. When he took you for his wife, he set you above all women, first in his thoughts and heart and home. That is a high place: a great distinction—the best a woman can have. You will not be unworthy of it?"

Patricia smiled drearily.

"You argue well, but would you speak like that if Frank had married you—out of compassion? Because he saw that you had given your affection unsought?"

"Love might begin that way," Nancy said hesitatingly, feeling the ground less sure under her feet. "I think there must always be one who cares most, and perhaps it is oftenest the woman. Men have such a much wider world. Yes, it might begin that way, while they were lovers still, and why not? But when two people are married—there is no tie like that of husband and wife. It must be either love or hate then, and you—you have been a woman crowned. Has he ever given you a look—said a word, to hurt you? Oh, child, think—think what you are throwing away when you put the gossip of a malicious, wicked old woman, who loves nothing in the world but to make mischief, before your husband's deeds. Has he not spoken by them?"

"He is kind," said Patricia, brokenly; "no one could be kinder. But ask yourself, Nancy, would it fill your heart—crown your days—to know that Frank would always be good to you, patient with you, kind to you, would even marry you, if no other, no lesser thing would make you happy? Ah yes, it might satisfy you till you found out; but if you were one day to know that his ideal woman was miles and miles above your head—that you could never come near her, do what you would—never make up to him for the loss of her?"

Nancy lifted her head with a proud gesture, her eyes alight.

"Do you think that I cannot be hurt, that you refuse to believe me?" she said. "I have told you the simple truth. There is nothing to conceal. Ask your husband, if you doubt me still. He is an honest man. He will tell you that, for a little while—before you came into his life, he tried to fan friendship into a warmer feeling, and failed. Is it fair to punish us both for a mistake? For you do punish us, Patricia; you insult an upright man, and a woman who has had no thought all her days but for one, no heart to give that was not given long, long ago."

"Ah, Nancy, do not think that I blame you, or—or Archie either. You cannot help being what you are, beautiful and good, and having loved the highest, how could he stoop to me? No, I am not saying it because I am humble. I am not a humble person. Do you think I want to make my days black and empty? Do you think I would accept the loss of everything, if I could cheat myself into thinking it all a foolish fancy?"

"But it is a foolish fancy, all the same," said Nancy, melting into tenderness once more for the poor wayward, misguided child, who was like to wreck her peace for a mere chimera, "a silly, silly fancy, which you will be the first to smile at when you come back to your own sane self. What does it all amount to? A tattler, a busybody, whom you have never seen or spoken to before, tells you some idle rumour about your husband's past, and you straightway pin your faith to her words, and forget every sign you have had of his tenderness for you. Isn't that foolishness? And besides, dear one, supposing it were all true, have we any right, we who are the chosen, to quarrel with the fancies our lovers may have had before our day broke? So long as we have the first place, so long as we cannot be dethroned, what does all else matter? Men are not as we—not as constant; we sit at home, and one image is enough to fill our thoughts. They move about the world and go into strange places, where there are always new faces, and some of them pretty faces, to stir a passing desire. If you and I had not been two secluded people, we might have sent our fancies roving too, before the real hero came upon the scene. Do you suppose "—she spoke with a smiling gaiety—" that if, when I am Frank's wife, I find some day that there were other girls whom he liked, who were kind to him when he was lonely, in London, and smiled on him—do you think, I say, that I should fall to crying and saying my life is ended and my joy dead and buried? Shall I not rather say, 'How proud I am that he has chosen me—

that he thought me the best'? And that is what you must say, my Patricia: you must say—oh, you will say it to-morrow, when we laugh over this panic of yours, 'I belong to my husband, and because I am his, I will not fall below the place he has given me; I will fill it as he would like me to fill it, by loving and trusting him, and thinking no evil of him.' That is what you will say, and to-night, when he comes home and you look in his face, you will be ashamed that you could ever think anything else !"

Patricia lifted her head and leaned back in the chair. She looked before her as if the warm, friendly words had passed her by, finding no entrance to her mind. Only the last of them left an echo in her ear.

"When I see him to-night," she said, facing a world in which there was left no single gleam of hope, "I shall know——"

The messenger sent for him had missed Sutherland, and he was late in reaching home. He jumped down from the dog-cart at the gate, and went in by the surgery door. He looked fagged and anxious. It seemed cruel to add to his burden.

"I've had a worrying day," he said, glancing up from the table where he was seated when I went in. "I hope you haven't come to send me to the other side of creation. What a dog's life it is!"

"No; there were one or two messages, but Butler has attended to them. Patricia isn't very well."

His worried frown changed to a look of concern.

"What's the matter?" he asked. "She was all right this morning."

"A nervous break-down, I fancy. Miss Gillespie is here; she has been with her all afternoon."

He got up, saying nothing, and went out of the room before me, but his face to me, who knew it so well, altered again in that instant; it wore the mask of cold reserve the mention of that name always drew over it.

Nancy had come out into the hall, and was waiting there.

" She had fallen asleep," she said to Sutherland, without any other word of greeting. Neither remembered that they had not met for months.

" In there ? "

" Yes ; she seemed so tired, I was afraid to disturb her."

He opened the dining-room door in his quick, quiet way, and went in alone. He stood looking down for a minute on Patricia, sleeping the sleep of exhaustion in his great chair. Her face was very pale, and there were dark rings under her closed eyes—she seemed scarcely to breathe. Her beauty was extinguished—but there was something pathetic in the childish helplessness of her attitude, as if sleep had overtaken her in the middle of a fit of passionate, unforgiven naughtiness.

He considered her critically, and, gently lifting her hanging hand, took account of her pulse. He looked perplexed when he came back to us, and the lines of worry had deepened on his brow.

" Will you come in here ? " he said courteously

to Nancy, leading the way to the drawing-room, " and tell me what she has been doing to herself. I can't make it out. She seems thoroughly run down."

He looked at me ; but I had nothing to tell, and it was Nancy who spoke. She said with straightforward directness—

" She went out after you left in the morning to leave a note for me. I had not got home then. On her way back she sat for a little in the churchyard ; Mrs. Laidlaw was there too, and went to her, and spoke to her. Something that was said disturbed Patricia. She has been over-wrought and agitated all afternoon."

" That old vixen ! " His tone showed deep annoyance. " She is enough to give any one a fever. Do you know what she said to upset Patricia ? "

Now, Nancy is like no other woman I have ever known—for it is her way to speak the simple truth without any thought of convention, or any of those decorations with which women love to drape the unpleasant. She looked tired, for even her abounding vigour had suffered from the afternoon's emotions, but a smile broke over her face—a smile of amused sympathy, as if she counted on and went halfway to meet his surprised incredulity.

"Mrs. Laidlaw is a clever woman," she said; "but this time I think she has been a little too clever, since she has tried to make your wife believe that you do not love her."

There was an instant's dead silence, in which the thuds of my own heart were like the sound of many waters in my ears.

Nancy looked at him, and her smile, seeing no answering smile meeting it, died away in a look of surprise that might merge into indignation, when he said, in clear emphatic tones—

"But I do love her."

He lied; but he lied bravely, and I, for one, honour him for it. It was the only way to save the situation.

"Of course," she said, a little austerely, as if she found some offence in his requiring to tell her this; "and to-morrow she will be the first to laugh at to-day's fears. But I know from experience," her mouth relaxed, "an unsought interview with Mrs. Laidlaw is very disastrous to the nerves."

"She's a scourge," he said, speaking in a measured sort of way; "but the mistake people make is in taking her seriously. She's a bully, and would be a coward if anybody snubbed her. Patricia isn't very strong, and I dare say she was frightened, poor child; but a night's rest will work wonders."

*   *   *   *   *

When she woke a little later, Archie was with her alone. I had gone to see Nancy home.

She looked up in his face in a wild, bewildered sort of way, put out her two hands, and then drew them back, shrinking from him.

"Come, and let me put you to bed, poor, tired, naughty child," he said.

She struggled, pushing him from her, and burst into wild cries and sobs.

He carried her to her room, and sat with her for hours, until the opiate he had given her took effect, and she fell into a deep sleep.

CHAPTER VII.

IT was the small hours of the night when Sutherland came to my room and threw himself into an easy-chair by the fire. He looked jaded and sombre. He felt with one hand along the mantelpiece for the matches, and lit his pipe before he spoke.

"She's asleep at last," he said.

"That's good hearing."

He stirred the coal with his foot till it gave out a sluggish flame.

"It's precious cold in your garret," he grumbled, with a shiver, "and only September, too."

"Have a whisky and soda."

He helped himself, and I waited for him to speak. After a time he said—

"A queer turn affairs have taken."

What was there to reply? The time to say anything that was worth while was long gone by.

"You heard what I said downstairs to-night?" He did not turn to me, but looked into the fire.

"To Miss Gillespie? Yes."

"It was not the truth."

"I knew it."

"All the same, I am not the villain you take me for," he said doggedly. "It is true I never made any pretence of loving Patricia in the way a man loves a woman when he tells himself he can't live without her. I don't know how it may be with other men, but I can't care twice in that way. But, God knows, since I made her my wife, I've never wronged her by so much as a thought. I wasn't going to play so low down as that—to marry one woman while I was secretly hankering after another. Patricia has had no rival since the day I asked her to be my wife; but, you see, I had nothing left to give her in the way of a grand passion."

"That was pretty rough on her."

"Why should it be?" he said irritably. "Haven't I done all that I promised? I undertook to make her happy, if I could—and I succeeded. You can't deny that I succeeded. But for that infernal old woman, and her meddling, would she have had a single ground of complaint? Has she any right now to complain?"

"I don't suppose she has complained."

"She looks and behaves as if her heart was broken, poor foolish child, and her life ruined. Ruined! Where's the difference in her lot that there should be all this mighty pother between this morning and now? I'm the same man she married—as ready to be kind to her, as anxious to please her; and because a gossiping old fool tells her I once cared for another woman——"

"Are you sure it was only once, Sutherland?"

He turned upon me sharply.

"On my word of honour," he said strongly, "I tell you again, from my wedding-day I've never thought of Miss Gillespie in the way a man thinks of the woman it is his supreme desire to marry. What I feel when I am with her is an echo of past emotion—of past pain. For all the rest she might be dead—is dead. She can never be quite the same to me as another, even if she's only a memory. I suppose the woman who first teaches a man the meaning of love must always have a place apart in his thoughts, but she is my wife's chosen friend, Harry—isn't that enough? Doesn't that define the position to satisfy you? It ought."

I know him for a man both strong and honourable. If he had set himself a difficult task, he had doubtless counted on his ability to carry it through, and justly enough. What he had not reckoned on was a force, stronger than his will, which he could not coerce. He had saved himself in Nancy's eyes, saved her the shame and bitter indignity of knowing herself preferred to her friend, the girl he called wife. He cared enough for Nancy still to spare her that insult to her pride and purity, but his bold, " And I do love her," which she had brushed aside impatiently as a wholly superfluous, almost ridiculous asseveration, could not deceive Patricia. Already, poor child, the veil had fallen from her eyes, and she knew herself unchosen. Sutherland and Nancy might be strong enough to front the difficulties in their path and overcome them; but the gay-hearted Patricia, was she to be crushed under the wheels of fate only because she had loved too impulsively?

" Say out what you think, man," he said, after a time; " you don't need to tell me you think I've been a fool, for your face says it."

" I think you're quite able to take care of yourself and your emotions; but Patricia— well, to be honest with you, I don't think you've dealt fairly by her."

" God knows I meant to do the best for her."

" You blame Mrs. Laidlaw——"

" Yes," he struck in, " you're right there. It's illogical, I admit that: she didn't create the situation, she only embellished it."

"I suppose when a man asks a woman in marriage, she is entitled to presume he offers her a devotion that isn't a mere sham."

"Do you think Patricia has any right to make that accusation?" he asked slowly.

"By your own showing, you had nothing but a kindly goodwill to offer her. A girl, where she gives her heart, asks for something more than that in return."

"Heaven alone knows what will content the heart of woman," he said, a little drearily. "I did my best. I thought we were getting on splendidly; I am very fond of her."

"You treat her like a child."

"And what is she, but a pretty, irresponsible child, to whom everything is to be forgiven? If she had been a sensible woman, we should have been spared these tears and lamentations. She would have seen through that old cat; have scorned her tittle-tattle."

"Sutherland, I think you are making a tremendous mistake."

"Oh, go ahead! I thought I had made all the blunders a man could make."

"You can retrieve this one, at any rate. You've laughed and jested with her, and it has answered well enough so far—so long as there was no cloud on the horizon. But she has wakened to her womanhood now; it is no longer an inexperienced schoolgirl you've to reckon with, but a woman, who has come into her inheritance of trouble. She won't be so ready to jest and be merry now, and you'll be wise if you cease to treat her as if she were a canary bird or a kitten—a mere pet and plaything."

"Women—most women, like—expect that kind of thing."

He was thinking of his mother, a silly woman, who could never remember she had grown up.

"I have so little time for home life," he defended himself, "and it seemed only fair to her youth to amuse her in the odd minutes. Why bother her with outside cares? I wanted to do what was fair, to give her all I could. But I dare say it was a big mistake. If I had let her alone, some other chap might have come along who would have satisfied her better, poor little woman. Marriage is a queer thing—a sea to which there is no chart; any minute you may wreck yourself on a sunken rock. And yet it seems an awfully simple thing — just to please one woman."

"So long as she's content to be fed on lollipops and compliments! But you can't keep her in pinafores for ever. Credit your wife with an intellect, and you'll find she has a very fair one; she has plenty of shrewd sound sense. You might do worse than advise with her."

"You ought to know. She owes a lot to you."

"She owes me simply nothing at all. It is I who have to thank her for a very pleasant companionship."

"Women in her condition are often hysterical," he said, staring into the fire as if to seek there the answer to his problem. "She'll be better when her child is born."

"Her child?"

"Yes. That will give her a fresh interest —a fresh hold—on life. It's the father—the husband—who is deposed then. After all, why shouldn't we jog along as well as others? The most devoted drift apart, sooner or later— or so it seems—and the least congenial learn to fit into each other's angles in time. It all comes to the same thing in the end. Ideals can't survive the marriage ceremony. One outgrows heroic passions, as one outgrows one's first dress-suit; but we may cultivate a steady, everyday, useable and workable sort of affection that wears better in the end."

He rose, and stretched himself, pushing the heavy hair back from his brow with a quick gesture, familiar to me when he was worried. He said he must snatch an hour or two of sleep if he was to be fit for his work next day. At the mention of work his face hardened into a more resolute purpose, the lines of annoyance a little effaced. It was clear that in work he looked to his safeguard, his compensation. Yet, before he slipped down to stretch himself on the little iron bed in the dressing-room, he was careful to remove his shoes, in fear lest the uneasy rest of the sleeper in the next room might be disturbed.

A little while ago he would not have spoken of marriage as a mere partnership, in which each member was bound to a certain tolerant forbearance; perhaps his character had suffered, as character must suffer when we willingly substitute the lower for the higher. Since he was capable of conceiving an ideal, it would have been better to stick to it, even at the cost of never realizing it, than to gratify his vanity by stooping to be kind. Since he had so little to give, would it not have been more truly generous to seem harsh, unsympathetic, uncomprehending, when Patricia made that girlish moan to him of her unhappiness, her loneliness?

Yet, to a man of his temperament, the temptation must have been great. The attainment of his own wishes was impossible. Never, if he lived to be a century old, could he hope to conquer so much as the outposts of Nancy Gillespie's affections; but here was a young, ardent creature, foolishly trusting, unspoiled by the world, with no taint of modern womanhood to tarnish her innocence; plainly nature had made her for a good house-wife, endowed her with every feminine art and charm. She would jingle the domestic keys with the most delightful importance, be wise and clever in her hospitalities, advise her children, look up to her husband as a lawgiver. And all these most excellent virtues might be his for the claiming; marvel of marvels, she cared for him—had given him her heart in her sweet, unreasoning, impulsive way. Would it be so very hard to like her, grow fond of her, to find a pleasure in pleasing her?

So he married her, forgetting that, since she was sole giver, it was she who ran the risks of the venture, and would be the only sufferer should it fail.

And he wondered that, while he was careful to set her in a pretty house, to give her every indulgence he could think of, pledged himself to take an interest in her frocks, her flowers, her household knicknacks—gave her honourable place as a rather valuable ornament to be handled tenderly, and admired and taken care of, she should suddenly waken into discontent.

She was like one who takes proud possession of an unexpected inheritance, and revels in the spaciousness and number of the rooms it is his lot to dwell in, till suddenly he discovers a wing to which there is no access, the entrance long since bricked up.

Behind that wall lay Sutherland's dreams, thoughts, remembrances, regrets.

But we who live in this workaday world cannot long remain at the high emotional level; a night's sleep, and we waken to the old prosaic views and wonder how it was that our pulses throbbed at fever speed, and our nerves betrayed us.

Sutherland came down next morning looking fresher for the few hours' rest a busy man can snatch at will, and able to eat a capital breakfast. Nothing particular seemed to have happened, except that we two were alone—it fell to me, as in old days, to pour out the tea.

Sutherland looked up for a moment, perhaps missing the dainty figure we had accustomed ourselves to see presiding there. Women are a very civilizing influence at the domestic board.

In answer to my question, he said she had had a good night and was better.

" I've advised her to keep quiet for a day or two," he said, looking straight at me. " I think she'll be all right soon. Perhaps when she gets round a bit she might like a little change. Do you happen to know—I haven't asked about their movements lately—do you think the Mortlakes are in town ?"

" I don't know for certain, but I should think it unlikely. We are scarcely at the end of September; he is sure to be shooting somewhere."

" Of course. My daily grind forgets to take note of an idle man's calendar. Well, then, there's Mrs. Tom; she's pretty certain to be in Kensington now, wherever Carnegie may be roving."

" Now that I think of it, she's been doing

some commissions for Patricia—some question
of needlework draperies to be designed, I
fancy——”

“She would like best to go and choose for
herself,” said Sutherland, with a lift of hope.
“It’s a great business for a woman, choosing
colours and matching shades, and so on.
We’ll get her sent off; I might manage to run
up with her myself if I could see the beginning
of an end to this measles epidemic. After all,
it must be deadly dull here for a girl, after
London. You and I have our work—or our
occupation, at any rate—but she has scarcely
had time to fit in yet.”

It was thus that we consciously skirted the
subject—wisely, I cannot but think. Sutherland could be confidential in a burst, the need
of an outpouring came at rare intervals—and
I, to whom he spoke, was like a second self—
safe as the walls of his private room. But he
could not go on talking over things as a
woman will—least of all a mischance such as
this. Even if he had been miserable, he would
have put an iron restraint upon himself, but

he was not miserable. Last night he had been impatient, irritable, almost hard; to-day it was plain he was hopeful things would yet right themselves somehow or other, and the sooner if they were not pawed over.

He spent the remainder of the half-hour allotted for breakfast in telling me of a new and daring adventure in surgery, that had taken great hold of him: he described it, animated wise, making a diagram of the tablecloth—here the victim, there the operator. The science of medicine, he said, was like groping in a dark room and hoping you might have the good luck not to stumble, but surgery was a rising sun, creeping between the shutters, with every hour growing brighter.

Once in the saddle, he dropped the cares of the husband and the lover like Christian's burden; he was nothing but the doctor, armed, his sword drawn to wage war against death and disease, yet he stopped on his way out to order a tray to be carried to Patricia's room, and himself put a flower upon it.

That was the man all over; he could be

thoughtful, mindful in little matters, yet would scarcely have let even the greatest interfere with his work. The people who suffer are the people who have no private refuge from disturbing moods.

Nancy came later, after Sutherland had seen his morning patients in the surgery and had ridden away. I saw her take the angle from Shaw Street, for I had established myself in the dining-room window, the forsaken nursery seemed too remote: I was a part of this household, and had a right to meddle with its troubles.

Nancy seemed to me to walk with a certain gravity, as if sad thoughts accompanied her, and insisted on contradicting the gaiety of her figure in the pink cotton gown, and the hat with roses which smacked of Edinburgh. She greeted me with a certain wistfulness, her eyes full of questions.

"Better," I said. "Go up to her; you'll do her more good than the beef-tea Archie prescribed at eleven. Did you ever know a doctor who didn't find in beef-tea a panacea for every ill under the sun?"

"I'll take it with me," she said, "in case she doesn't find me medicinal. Do you know, I can never remember being ill in my life except once, long, long ago, when I had whooping-cough, and that was half play."

"Then you are one of the happy people who can eat grapes and jelly without disturbing reminiscences. I wonder what you would do if you were really ill?"

"Get better," she said, with a smile. "We give in too easily. Half the time we might conquer Fate when we let it subdue us."

Here, if anywhere, was one who could help Patricia in her uphill struggle. It seemed to me, as the one who looked on, that there was something rather fine in this close union between two who might so easily have been rivals. It betokened a certain nobility and honesty of purpose in each.

"You held my husband's heart." "You supplanted me in a lover's fancy." This might have been the language of jealousy, but there was no room in either nature for such smallness. The weaker instinctively clung to the stronger, finding shelter and support in that quality which, for lack of a better definition, we call common sense Nancy could be depended on to take the sane and the sober view; to think at least wisely for others, however sadly to us she might seem to misspend her own chances.

She came down from Patricia's room in an hour's time: I had heard a footstep overhead, and once a laugh that had good cheer in it.

She came in, her fine mouth smiling.

"She has taken every drop of the beef-tea," she said brightly. "I thought you would like to know."

"That's your magic."

"I'm afraid I must share the honours with the cook. It really had a most appetizing smell."

"Oh, we let the nurse have all the glory in these cases."

"Yet the nurse is powerless unless she's backed by the doctor. I told Patricia her husband wished her to take it, and she obeyed at once."

" Like a good sensible lass."

" Patricia is very reasonable. She was a little upset yesterday, but of course every one is at times, even you, I think, though you always look so cool and unperturbed."

" Even my majestic calm might be shattered under the shock of encounter with Mrs. Laidlaw."

" I don't think she matters," said Nancy, straightening herself with a lift of her shoulders that had the effect of haughtiness.

This was our way of telling each other that our tragedy was not to be considered tragic. We were to look it in the face, and pass it by unrecognized. Poor little bruised heart up-stairs; your grief, your dignity, were in safe enough keeping.

" Must you go ? " I asked. " Hadn't you better come back to administer the next dose of slops ? Patricia has reduced me to such a condition of abject slavery that my authority goes for nothing."

" I'll come as soon as I can, but this is Sophia Green's wedding-day, and I am bidden.

Didn't you notice my finery? Patricia approves. She says Edinburgh is not more than four weeks behind the decrees of London; that is very comforting to our provincial souls. The marriage is to be in church—an innovation Shawbridge doesn't quite know in what spirit to accept. It's fashionable, but some people find texts to discountenance it!"

"A case of wresting Scripture——"

"I think so. Papa is to—I was going to say preside, you would understand if you saw the church!—to officiate, and I must go home and see that his bands have the proper degree of starch."

She spoke with less of evenness than usual, more volubly than was her way, as if something troubled her she wished to hide.

She turned at the door.

"I wish you were coming," she said; "but I suppose you haven't been asked?"

"No. But would a humble corner in the gallery be forbidden?"

"Do come," she said cordially. "I will tell Roger, our beadle, to keep a seat for you.

I wish," she smiled humorously, "I could be up there with you. I shall hate being in the middle of that crowd, saying polite things. I think I was meant to look on at life."

"From a height?"

"One can look on from the struggling level too," she said, hurrying away.

Yes, preside was the word; no lesser would suffice to characterize the attitude of the imposing priestly figure, towering above the background of palms and gay exotics. Shawbridge was in great conceit of its minister that day. He wore his black Geneva gown with an air; it was of corded silk, a gift from the ladies of the congregation; he had a hood too—had not the ancient University of St. Andrews, in a moment of weak enthusiasm, bestowed on this ornament of the Kirk the right to its purple and white? A woman with rusty black flowers in her bonnet leaned across me to whisper to a friend—

"A braw figure of a man."

Even here, among the uninvited, he had his disciples.

The mill girls, loosed at the dinner-hour, with whom I shared the back gallery, were loud in their criticism of the gowns and gew-gaws; a restless, crimson patch—Genoa velvet, according to these same authorities—indicated Mrs. Whittlemore, very large, very important; others of the privileged were nearly as gay. Somehow, in all this flashing of colours and of jewels, and fragrance and opulence of flowers, the bride seemed to be eclipsed.

She looked slight and insignificant; she had grown thin, a mere peg upon which to hang so many yards of costly white satin. She stumbled when she came up the aisle on the arm of her bluff and conscious father; he held it at an acute angle, and her finger-tips scarcely seemed to rest upon it—as if at any moment she might cease her hold and turn and fly. He looked ill at ease, in his white waistcoat and holiday orchid, but his mouth was set grimly. She had played the last of her pranks, poor prisoner, and there was no escape for her now.

Perhaps I misread the scene; it is a tradition with maidens to weep and seem reluctant on the wedding-day, and perhaps Miss Sophia had neither been coerced nor cajoled into consent; perhaps, in her shallow little heart she was even proud of her capture —a "little shilpet thing," as some one called her, to secure so big a prize in the marriage lottery. Happily, the bridegroom looked no stern jailor; a homely figure, with little outward sign of his millions; prematurely old and bald, somewhat yellow and wrinkled, perhaps, with the oppression of making money and the care of keeping it to take a young girl's fancy, but a plain, good sensible face. Sophia Green had good reason to hope for an indulged, care-free life.

In a very little while she was Sophia Blythe, and all her friends in a bustle congratulating each other. Her happiness they took for granted when they kissed her cheek—white as the satin of her gown— with the kiss of approval. She had done the right thing, and now she was meeting with her reward — rather a " shauchling," parchment-coloured reward, but oh, so rich! Some people—a good many, perhaps—envied her; no one was sorry for her. The time for pity, and lamentations, and tears was six short weeks later, when Hugh Blythe was found dead in his bed, and the bridal finery was exchanged for crape.

CHAPTER VIII.

PATRICIA made no moan; did not obtrude her troubles. Her good blood and breeding, inherited from several generations of self-restrained, well-mannered people, stood the test to which it had been suddenly subjected; after that one outburst of hysterical weeping, there were no more tears, no more laments; not even to Nancy did she again lay bare her soul. In that little interval of seclusion, when she nursed the conventional headache, she had faced her future and braced herself to meet whatever it might require of her.

Her hurt was grievous; her disillusionment complete; but the pride of race and of nature rose in defence. She must live to fight, to endure; light her little candles of friendship and comfort herself by their glimmer since the sun of her life had gone down. And perhaps, all unknown to herself, the future, unrelieved by any ray from heaven as it seemed, was not all hopeless. Youth cannot realize perpetual defeat; something must happen, some crisis must arise beyond which may lie new conditions; so the heart cheats itself even when it abandons itself to despair.

"I have been ill, you know," she said, that first day, when she came downstairs, wrapped in a white shawl, "and Nancy has been nursing me; but I am better, Friend; I am not going to be ill any more."

"That's good news. Indeed, my dear, I was beginning to think that you were encroaching on my privileges. I have so long been the only chartered invalid in this house that I take very badly indeed with a rival. When I smelt that beef-tea, I felt myself ill used."

"You shall be my patient next time, and have all the beef-tea," she said. "It is ever so much nicer to be the nurse, one can be so autocratic. I have been studying Nancy's methods, and I shall know just how to treat you. Oh, here comes Nancy——"

"Speak of the fox and his tail appears," said Nancy, gaily; "that's the rendering of the proverb I prefer. And how are you to-day, my patient? and what business have you to be down here without my permission?"

"I've given up the rôle of patient. Friend Fowler says it is an infringement of his rights. I've been telling him I shall know just the proper amount of severity to mingle with my mercy when he falls into my hands. I rather wish"—she looked at me with a brave attempt at the old gaiety—"that you would develop a mild complaint—engrossing, but not too serious; it would be something to do."

"Thank you; but I'm not in any particular lack of occupation."

"But I am, it seems. Nancy has been lecturing me; she has taken shameful advantage of my helplessness; she knew I couldn't fight. She says I'm too idle. I thought I'd been very busy. I have called on every callable-on-woman in Shawbridge, and I have made my house pretty; there's nothing more to do for it, unless I dismantle it and begin all over again."

"Alas for the day when woman was allowed to consider the house her kingdom! Furnish over again! Good heavens! Why, Burton never even subjected us to the indignity of a spring cleaning."

"Oh, I know! Mrs. Tom Carnegie described the cobwebs; she said she smuggled in a charwoman on the pretext that her maid required a chaperon! Imagine any woman needing to be protected from Burton! But don't be afraid. I'm going to rest satisfied with my kingdom as it is. My decorations must be allowed to soak—seep is your word, isn't it?—to seep into the mind of Shawbridge before I continue its education. It is one satisfaction in life to have the only harmonious drawing-room in the place. My

energies must find another outlet since Nancy
will have it that I must work."

"Oh, there's heaps to do!" said Nancy
lightly. "If I were a proper daughter of
the Manse, I would enlist you for parish
work ; but papa has always set his face
against that sort of thing." Her own brave
face never changed. "But there's me, for
instance—I want new things—lots of things.
When I was in Edinburgh a dressmaker told
me that, while I had always been clothed, I
had never been dressed! Think of living
to my age to make such a discovery as that.
There's a big field for you!"

"A mission after my own heart—the dress-
ing of Nancy!"

In this way we bridged the chasm, and
hid away in our hearts the fears that were
knocking there.

One could but second Patricia's efforts, so
pluckily made, and help her to help herself.

Often in the mornings she would come to
my room, with a very needless apology for
disturbing me.

"It's so dull alone," she would say. "If you don't mind, I'll sit a little with you—I won't bother you. See, I've brought my book, too!"

But it was another Patricia who sat in the big chair—no longer sentencing herself to the stool of penitence; it would almost seem as if she had grown too old for levities of that order. She was, indeed, older; the gaiety which had been so spontaneous was a put-on thing now, and often she seemed to forget to make the effort, and would grow silent and grave again in the middle of a jest. A woman looked out of the eyes where the spirit of a child had dwelt before.

"You don't seem very much interested in your historian," I said one day, seeing her turn over the leaves of a tattered yellow-back with a hairpin, and every now and then let it fall in her lap while she looked in front of her. "Isn't he setting forth his tale properly?"

"I'm afraid I haven't been paying atten-tion," she said, colouring faintly. "I have a wandering mind. It looks as if it had cheered a good many solitary meals, doesn't it?—and not gone without its share?"

"That's what you must expect if you sit at the same literary board with all the mill hands of Shawbridge."

"I was thinking of what you once said—or was it I who suggested it?—about collecting a library of my own. It might be amusing."

"A capital idea. It was to be composed of shilling shockers, wasn't it, with bindings to match their lurid contents?"

"Was I ever so silly as that?"

"Be silly now. It becomes you."

But she would not smile.

"I was considering," she went on, not heeding my nonsense, "whether it mightn't be worth while to try and educate myself—or uneducate myself. The useless lumber my governesses carried about with them is rather shabby furniture, but then I never encouraged them to provide anything better. I wish you'd tell me what books to begin with."

"I can only tell you what I like and have found useful myself."

"Yes," she hesitated, "I suppose your tastes, and those of any educated, intelligent man would be the same?"

"To say yes to that would be obvious self-praise, wouldn't it?"

"You know what I mean—there must be some standard by which men judge of other men's and women's cultivation."

"Of course there are certain main lines every decently-educated person is supposed to travel over, but when he has got beyond the common ground, a man generally chooses —or somehow or other falls upon his own particular by-way. I like rooting and grubbing about among the bones of the past; Archie, of course, concerns himself chiefly with the newest developments and discoveries in his own branch of science; but if his reading is all professional now, it wasn't so once. He was fond of what somebody has called 'fine, miscellaneous literary feeding.'"

"What did he read—do you remember?" she asked, with quickened interest.

Not long before, when I moved my quarters, I had come across a chest full of old favourites of his, stowed away in a garret to make room on his shelves for the newest treatises on disease. I made a selection from these, rejecting some that did not tend to edification, and had them neatly arranged on a spare shelf before she next visited me. She took them out one by one, and looked at them gravely.

"Do you mind my keeping them up here?" she asked.

"If you don't think it a trouble to come upstairs, we might look into them together," I answered. "I find I am awfully rusty too—one thinks one knows a thing, but it's possible for it to get buried pretty deep."

"Thank you," she said gravely. "I knew I could count on you. You see, it isn't for myself; but I mustn't be too ignorant, for the sake of—another."

Not husband, but the child to be born to her was in her thoughts.

"My baby must not grow up to despise its mother. I shall not again make the mistake of thinking that to love enough is everything. It is just nothing—nothing at all. If I had been clever or accomplished, I might have made Archie forget that he had ever cared for any one grand and big-natured, like Nancy," ran the bitter thought. " I might have made him content with me; but I had nothing to give him but a heart, and that he never coveted."

If the change was apparent in the wife, it was no less marked in the husband, though each controlled it more or less successfully in the other's presence. Archie's careless confidence in all being well was shaken. In the first months of his married life, beyond being thoughtful of her comfort and indulgent to her whims, he had troubled himself very little about his wife; he certainly had not spent a single hour in analyzing her possible feelings. He would have laughed at the absurdity if any one had suggested such a thing. If he had been questioned, he would have said unhesitatingly that his marriage had answered admirably.

And so he might have continued to think till the end of his life, complacent over the success of his experiment and utterly ignorant that she had any rights, or wants, or needs beyond those he supplied—but for that strange and sudden upheaval of nature's placid surface, revealing the unsuspected depths beneath.

Its immediate effect was to make him irritable, as a man is when the domestic peace is threatened. He fell into the common error of thinking Patricia unreasonable because she failed to fit his preconception of her; it took a little longer to persuade him that the original mistake had been his own.

But at least he could no longer dismiss his home with careless unconcern from his mind when he rode from the door; for the first time since his hasty engagement, he took account of her seriously, as a human creature with impulses and needs and desires of her own.

Often and often I would see him watch her furtively, as if he could not reconcile himself to the change in her. She was unfailingly gentle in her manner, she tried to throw off her languor—for her moods alternated between listlessness and fits of restlessness—when with him, and would listen and answer, and volunteer her own little items of news, but the old blithe spirit was gone, the old gay sparkle quenched: nobody could accuse her of being impulsive now.

"It's her health," he said, looking at me eagerly one day, as if he challenged me to deny it. "She'll be her old self again by-and-by. She's so young."

He was sitting alone in his room; he looked worried and fagged.

"She doesn't seem ill, she goes about a great deal. She and Miss Gillespie seem to find plenty to do."

"Too much, perhaps, women have no moderation. I must interfere if she gets overdone."

"Don't restrict her too much. It's an interest—an occupation. She is very energetic by nature."

"Then you think she's in pretty good

spirits?" he said anxiously; "you see so much more of her than I do, Harry. It's odd to have to come to my friend for news of my wife; but—there it is! She always declares she's perfectly well when I ask her, but I don't want her to worry. It's bad for her just now."

"She's cheerful enough," I said, to comfort him, "and always busy. She's become a great reader, and she runs about, in and out with Nancy, or goes into the Free Manse to talk to the old minister. They've become great friends."

"It's I who am the wet blanket," he said, with a dreary smile. "I dare say she's bright enough when we're apart. I shouldn't mind anything, Harry, if—if she didn't seem half afraid of me. That cuts me—I haven't deserved it."

"Oh, nonsense, man! That's just your imagination. You see next to nothing of her till the evening, when she's tired, and you say yourself that it isn't to be expected she should be in rampant spirits."

"Please God, she'll be her old merry, careless self when she has her child in her arms," he said, joining his hands behind his head and staring in front of him. "It's a dreadful thing, Harry, old man, to think you've robbed any young creature, however unwittingly, of even a share of her right to be happy."

"It's for you, not for her child, to win her back," I dared to say, a hand on his shoulder; but my heart was sore for him, for I knew he had no easy task before him.

"That old demon has sent for me," he said, with an impatient change of subject. His irritable frown came back. "She's ill."

Of course he could mean no other than Mrs. Laidlaw.

"What will you do?"

"Professionally, I've no choice. Black won't go near her. It's a matter—as a medical man—of turning the other check. But there's Patricia to consider, and what she might feel."

"I think one may feel pretty sure what she'll say."

"I begin to think I shall never be able to predict what a woman may do or feel. She may fancy I'm in league with the old fiend."

"Why don't you go and ask her? She's alone in the drawing-room."

That was the way of it now: she in one room, he in another; a little while before she would have rebelled had he shut himself away for a whole evening, and now he went to her half reluctantly, as if it were he who was afraid.

"Of course," said Patricia, evenly, when the question had been put to her, "if she is ill and requires you, you must go to her, must you not? You do not," she added, with a faint smile, "consult me about your patients, as a rule."

The vivid flush that name had brought to her cheek, had died away, leaving her very pale. She had on her hat and gloves, and stood at the table. He was keeping her waiting; he had an odd feeling that he was being granted an interview and must make speed.

"If you've any feeling about it——" he said awkwardly.

"Why should I?" she asked quietly, woman-like, far more mistress of the situation than he. "I don't care for Mrs. Laidlaw personally, but that describes my feelings towards a good many of your patients, and it certainly would not hinder you from attending them profession-ally. Will you have coffee before you go out?"

"Patricia," he said hoarsely, "you wouldn't have answered me like that once."

"I am learning better, you see. I dare say I was very unreasonable about the patients at first. I see it now. I believe," with a little laugh, "I thought you might keep them waiting if—if there was anything nicer to do at home."

"I would do it now, if you asked me."

"Ah, but I have learned my lesson better than that! And besides, there's nothing so nice as work. I have found that out too. If you don't mind—and there is nothing else you wanted to say—I think I shall go now." She glanced at the clock.

"Out—so late as this? It is quite dark."

"I promised to sit with Mr. Cunningham for half an hour. The evenings are so long for him. Mary can go with me—if you don't object."

"Have I ever objected to anything that gave you pleasure?" he said, with annoyance. "But I can't have you going along that dark road with only another girl for protection. I will take you myself."

"She will learn some day that I am not a taskmaster," he thought. "If she chooses to be unhappy, at least it will not be because I thwart her."

But his irritability was increasingly difficult to rein in. She was punishing him needlessly for what was, after all, no such serious offence. Many a better-loved woman had a less devoted husband than he was prepared to be. If she expected impossibilities in the way of sentiment, she had only her schoolgirl gaze at life to blame for the disappointment. But, argue as he might, their strained relations fretted him.

She yielded passively while he drew her hand within his arm. He said to himself, grimly, he ought to be grateful that she did not shrink from him. Once, when she stumbled at a crossing, he felt her hand tighten its grasp, and it gave him a queer thrill. He drew her closer.

"You're not hurt?" he asked, in a concerned voice.

"No," she said faintly, thinking, poor child, how despicable it was of her—how poor a surrender of her pride, to feel her heart bound and throb at the first softening of his tone.

"I'll come for you as soon as I can get away," he said. "You mustn't get tired—and poor old Cunningham isn't able for much now."

"Is there really no hope?" she asked.

"I fear not. He has been getting weaker for months. It's only a question of time."

Her silence expressed her sorrow; the once gay Patricia had few words now. He felt for her in losing this new friend; but he found no word of comfort to say.

As he left her at the Manse door and walked away, he missed the timid touch of her hand on his arm. He felt himself longing —to his own surprise—for some manifestation of the tenderness that would once have bored him.

CHAPTER IX.

IT must have been a thing to see Sutherland with Mrs. Laidlaw! The one enemy whom that redoubtable old woman could not face had come into her dingy bedroom, taken possession there, and would not be ejected. She was no more valiant than another when pain had her in its grip, and indeed, like all bullies, she was cowardly under personal suffering.

Charlie Nairn was in the dining-room when Sutherland was shown in there by the frightened-looking maid. Charlie was not frightened—not he! The tyrant who had dispensed so many lectures there was a prisoner upstairs; and the garrulous youth was sipping a glass of her famous port with all the nonchalance in the world.

"Have a drink?" he said to Sutherland, hospitably pushing the decanter across the dingy cloth. "It isn't every day you'll get the chance. My! If old McAlister was caught forgetting the keys when the old lady was about, wouldn't she just get her head snapped off? But she's upstairs, blubbing over her dear mistress!" He mimicked pretty successfully the tone of the foolish, kindly creature, whose soft heart was so easily touched.

"Take care, Charlie," said Sutherland, unable to help smiling at the boy's airs; "if you follow Mrs. Laidlaw's practices, you'll inherit her penalties. If she hadn't looked on the port when it was red, there would have been no gout for me to cure now."

"It's precious few chances I get of seeing the colour of this or any other wine here," said Charlie, filling up his glass with a flourish; "and, you bet, I ain't going to turn modest and say 'No,' when it's put under my very nose. What's gout?"—with infinite scorn. "Hoots, man, you needn't try to frighten me with that bogey!"

"You won't say 'What's gout?' when you're under the thumbscrew, Charlie, my boy."

"Thumbscrew, eh?" said Charlie, briskly. " It scrunches then, and grinds and burns ?"

" A red-hot poker is nothing to it."

" Ha ha!" laughed Charlie, with malicious glee. " And it ties a body by the heels so that they can't escape, and it tears and it aches, and it twists and it screws, till they've got to yell out with the pain of it, and they can't sleep, and they've got to live on slops, and take beastly medicine."

" A fairly accurate picture. See what you're coming to ! "

" Me ! See what *she's* come to ; and serve her right ! Hasn't she made it hot enough for others ? I tell you what, she should have lived in the days of the martyrs she's so fond of making old McAlister read about on Sundays. Wouldn't she just have been a jolly

old persecutor? Talk of the rack! It wouldn't
have been good enough for her. She'd have
wanted to do like those old Roman beggars,
and chuck a fellow into a pot full of boiling
oil, or see him frizzle on a gridiron. That
would have suited her down to the ground.
And now she's in for it herself. I say "—he
stopped suddenly and looked at Sutherland
sideways, with a knowing wink—" you said
you were going to *cure* her, didn't you?
Good joke that, eh?"

"I'm going to do my best," said Sutherland,
pleasantly; "and, as I don't want to have
another patient on my hands, I'm going to
lock this up—by your leave." He lifted the
decanter.

"A beastly mean thing to do," said Charlie,
turning sulky.

"I promise you shall have another bottle,
fresh opened, to drink to Mrs. Laidlaw's
restored health," Sutherland smiled sardoni-
cally; "and meantime I know you'll be glad
to smuggle the sideboard keys to poor Miss
McAlister's room before they're missed. She's

done you many a good turn—more, perhaps, than you know of—in this house. And you don't want to get a woman into trouble, do you?"

In the sick-room he found the witless companion weeping futile tears, and trembling under the storm of threats and abuse that raged within the big tent-bed. In her hours of suffering Mrs. Laidlaw fell back upon the language of a robuster age.

Sutherland paused behind the faded damask curtains, drawn close to hide the light. He was unseen by the patient; but Miss McAlister heard him enter, and looked up with a little cry of dismay.

"Oh, doctor, doctor!" she said, under her breath, putting out her hands in a frightened way as if to ward him off.

"The doctor, is't?" said a voice from behind the drapery, imperious still, unquelled by pain. "What for are ye hiding him, ye eediot? Do ye think I sent for him to cure you of the hysterics? 'Deed, an' it would baffle the whole faculty to put a grain of sense in your pow! Draw the curtain, and take yourself out of the road, ye gomeral."

Then Sutherland found himself alone with her, looking down on her grim, pain-distorted face. The dauntless, beady black eyes met his searchingly.

"So ye've come?" she said.

"Didn't you send for me?"

"Ay, that did I; but it wasna' to say ye would come at my bidding. They telled me ye was a mettlesome lad."

"I'm a doctor. Any one who suffers, and whom I can relieve, has a right to expect my services."

"You bit lady wife of yours would maybe teach ye another tune, if ye consulted her."

"My wife?" he said serenely. "What has she got to do with the fact of your calling me in professionally? A doctor's wife has nothing whatever to do with his patients."

He would have died sooner than let her guess that she had struck at the root of his happiness; to have disclosed Patricia's sufferings to the woman who had purposely caused them, would have been an impossible in-decency. Patricia's pride had carried her triumphantly through that interview in the churchyard; only after it was over, and she in the safe shelter of her room, did she break down. His own scorn forbade him, by so much as a twitching muscle, to betray his wounds.

She gave a cackling laugh.

"McAlister was feared ye would poison me. Ye saw for yourself she was fair scunnered at the sight of you."

"That would be incorrect treatment for gout," he said, with unabated courtesy, ignoring her meaning. He glanced at the bandaged foot, laid for coolness outside the bedclothes. "You have had a pretty sharp attack?"

As he spoke, a fresh paroxysm of pain came on. She seized his arm with a grip of iron; her face changed from its habitual expression of cunning malice, to one of terror and blind dread. For him, as never for another, the mask was removed, and all her craven soul laid bare.

"Doctor, doctor!" she screamed. "Save me! save me! an' I'll never say ill word of you or yours while there's ony breath left in my body. I'm feared to die—I'm no' ready yet. They say I'm an ill-tongued auld wife; but dinna' you believe them. My bark's waur than my bite." Her Scotch accent grew more pronounced with her excitement. "Eh, but it's the Evil One himsel' that's clawin' at me! It's past bearing! I'm just in the grup of mortal pain, and ye stand there glowering at me, ye donnered deevil! Doctor, doctor! can ye no' do onything for me? Would ye see me die, an' no' lift a finger to save me?—me that could buy Shawbridge twice over? No, no—what am I saying? I'm just fair demented wi' the pain. I'm no' that rich—no' near sae rich as folks tell ye; but there's a pickle siller in the bank. I'll give it ye—every bawbee of it'll be yours, if ye'll ease me of this weary, weary pain!"

He was doing what he could for her, heedless of her clamour and outcry, and when she gained some relief she sank back exhausted.

"Ye'll no mind me," she said, almost anxiously, when she could speak again. " Ye'll no take offence at a sick woman's whimsies. I'm hearing ye're a poor man, with nothing laid by for a rainy day, and the road to fortune's a stey brae to climb. Listen!"— she looked round furtively. "The door's steeket? Ay, McAlister would never dare to come ben unbidden. Listen!"—she spoke in a sibilant whisper. "Cure me, set me on my feet again to rule my ain house, an' I'll make ye rich. My money's my own; there's no' a soul that can lay claim to it, though there's many a one that'll smile on the wrong side of his mouth when he finds he's no' set down in my will. Ye needn't tell me you're proud. I can see it fine in your face; but, man, if I've read ye right, and I ken something of human nature, ye would rather earn the siller from me in the honest exercise of your profession than be beholden for every bite and sup ye put between the lips to the wife ye married for her money, and who kens it."

He looked at her, unable to keep the scorn

out of his eyes. She turned uneasily on the pillow. Never before had she stooped to beg, to bribe, to beseech for the life that might at any moment be extinguished. The fiery anguish had laid hold of her side and shoulder as well as her foot—if it attacked the heart she was doomed.

"I will do my best for you, as for any other patient, because it is my business to save even a vicious life," he said sternly; "but, understand once for all, I will never defile my hands with money of yours. Neither in the shape of fee nor of legacy."

"Sirce me," she said, still anxious to cajole, "but you're ill to please, doctor! Am I no' telling ye to make your own charge, an' I'll meet it blithely? There's mony a one would jump at that chance."

"Perhaps," he said coldly; "but I am not one of them. I am going to ring for your companion; if you have anything more to say it must be said before her. But I advise you to keep quiet; you will get sooner well."

She looked at him with a scrutiny that felt

itself baffled. It was difficult, almost impossible, for her to believe that he could spurn her offer and yet give her fair play. She measured him, as she measured all the world, by her own standard. When she sent for him she held him bribable. He was said to be clever—too good for Shawbridge; but he was dependent on his profession, and she was in mortal need. Her pride went down before the assaults of pain. Perhaps it was natural he should resent her freedom of speech, her efforts to alienate his wife; but she conceived of no affront or injury that money would not heal. Let him but relieve her and he should be paid royally.

And he looked at her and flung her offers back in her face. Why had he come? Why did he look at her with such absolute indifference when she hinted at her trespasses against him, and almost stooped to ask his pardon? "I told her he had married her for her money, and her fine family, maybe, thinking they would help him to rise, but never for love of her, as the silly quean believed." Was it possible her shafts had not sped home, after all ? Could it really be that these young folks cared enough for each other to look on her endeavour to separate them as a pretty jest, a good joke to laugh at in private ? Even while he was attending to her, he said carelessly to McAlister—

" My wife will be waiting for me ; I left her at the Free Church Manse, and promised to call for her and take her home."

A pang of rage shot through her, as she thought that, after all, her plot might have failed. She had desired to be revenged on Fowler and on Nancy by striking at them through their friends, and was she to be the only sufferer ? The next instant the miserable old woman was cowering and shivering in the clutch of a new dread. She was helpless in this man's hands ; all the resources of science were at his call ; he was incorruptible, not to be seduced by gift or flattery. If he chose to punish her, who in all the wide world could she count on to save or defend her ? But one poor soul had any lingering survival of affection for her, and she was little better than a fool.

He laughed with a kind of bitter amusement when he left the house.

"She suspects me of using my chances to rid Shawbridge of its incubus! She dreads my acquaintance with drugs! A whiff or a sip of some stuff, and there might be an end of her!" What a pleasantry that might have been to carry home if—if Patricia and he had been another manner of husband and wife. But confidence between them was slain.

"If I could have lied to Patricia too." But his whole soul rose in revolt at the very thought of that perjury; he had not loved her, and the truth and its bitter consequences were easier to face than the immeasurable scorn she would have meted out to his falseness.

He began to hate Shawbridge, where he had fought so hard for a victory only to have the taste of success taken out of his mouth before he knew its flavour. Nothing was going right. The patient whose life had flowered into holiness was leaving him, and a pernicious, poisonous human weed like Mrs. Laidlaw revived to flourish and sting anew.

She made an excellent recovery, and as danger grew more remote, the magnitude of her own generosity confounded her. She pointed out to Sutherland, dreading that he would think better of his folly, that the words of a woman silly with pain need not be taken too literally, and that Tom Nairn had always considered it an honour to attend her for nothing ; but she was grateful enough for his " spunk," when she was at last persuaded he really meant to refuse the offers pressed upon him in her panic, to say, with half-jesting apology, in her broadest doric—

" I'll no' deny that my tongue's an unruly member, and that whiles it rins awa' wi' me ; but, sirce me, doctor, if ye had lived all your life amang sic a set of sumphs, no' to say sycophants, each more ready than the other to bend and to boo, ye would turn randy-wife yoursel' for fair weariness an' need o' diversion."

" Perhaps I should," he answered drearily. He had come to a pass when it was possible to believe that in a life out of which all the savour and pleasure had been squeezed one might even fall so low as this.

Ours was not a bright home in those dark, short days of gloomy winter. Sutherland came home from his rounds too fagged to make much effort to talk ; often we smoked for an hour or more in unbroken silence, when Patricia, making an excuse of her weariness, went early to bed. There was nothing to break the monotony ; people grew tired of asking us to dinners which we persistently refused to eat, and we had not energy enough to imitate our fellow-townsfolk, who found livelier entertainment in the theatres and concert-halls of Edinburgh.

To the amazement of Shawbridge, Nancy suddenly developed a taste for society, and appeared at every local function by her father's side. The spiteful said it was to show off the new dresses the doctor's wife encouraged her vanity to wear, setting her up in the last London fashions ; even the more charitable wondered how, after her many professions of attachment to Mr. Cunningham, she could leave him in his extremity to be nursed by a stranger. Caprice and fickleness were greater vices than vanity.

Nancy said nothing, perhaps cared nothing, but she accepted all the notes of invitation for herself and her father, put on her finery, stoically faced the many courses between the two kinds of soup and the hothouse grapes that illustrate Shawbridge hospitality, and even, at much toil to herself and Ann, made return feasts at the Manse.

Thus winter crawled by with leaden feet, and in March there was that stirring of Nature's pulse that whispers of the earth's re-birth; a tinge of green overlay the hedgerows, so long brown and sere; against the sky the swelling buds tipping the tree twigs could be discerned. By the time the leaves were uncurled there would be a new piece of life to brighten our dull house—with the coming of the little one the shadows would surely rise; baby hands must needs draw these estranged hearts together.

But Patricia's child only lived two days. The old man was spared yet a little longer, but the Angel of Death, winging towards the Manse, had claimed tithe of us by the way.

*   *   *   *   *

She said very little when they told her the feeble breath had fluttered out. She asked to see the baby, and lay looking at it for a long time, resting as if in sleep within the circle of her arm. Archie was with her, and when he looked sorrowfully down on the little waxen face, she involuntarily drew the small burden closer to her, as if even in her grief she refused him any share.

His heart ached with pity for her, his own suffering forgotten.

He put his cheek down beside hers with a rare movement of tenderness.

"My poor child," he said brokenly, "I would have given anything, done anything to spare you this, if I could."

She said nothing for a moment, then turned her head aside, perhaps that he might not witness her emotion.

"I am glad—glad she didn't live," she whispered. "A boy would be different—he could defend himself; but a girl—she would only grow up to make mistakes and—and suffer for them. Oh, I wish—I wish I had died too!" she broke into sudden cries and sobs.

Sutherland never left her side for twenty-four hours, an anxious time for all of us, waiting, unable to help; he came out of the sick-room looking haggard and ten years older, and I alone stood mourner by that tiny grave.

"The child?" he said roughly, when some one spoke of the interment. "It's past hurting. It's the mother we must think of, if she's to live."

"Mrs. Sutherland will do nicely now," said the distinguished Edinburgh physician, over a glass of wine which I dispensed in the consulting-room. "With a little care and prudence," he continued blandly, "there is really no occasion for further anxiety. Her husband has been terribly concerned—almost needlessly so, if I may say so; but we bachelors, Mr. Fowler, are perhaps scarcely fitted to sympathize with, or even to comprehend, such a situation."

But even a week later, when Lady Mortlake descended unexpectedly upon us, Patricia had made no great progress, and Sutherland insisted on preparing her before allowing the visitor to go to her.

He did not look particularly cordial when he found his mother-in-law in possession—perhaps anticipating an increase of his difficulties. The cloud had fallen upon him again with the child's death; for it seemed as if his last hope of reconciliation was buried in that little grave.

"The dear child did not ask me to be with her in her illness," Lady Mortlake confided in me, to whom it fell to entertain her. "And really it was most considerate; for she knows how nervous I am, and so foolishly sensitive! I am absolutely useless in an invalid's room—of quite too emotional a temperament to be a good nurse. Haven't you noticed how hard and self-contained the professional nurse is ? But perhaps you are one of the strong people who are lucky enough to have no experience of sickness ? No ; Patricia, dear girl, understood that I must deny myself the luxury of watching over her at the crisis, and spared me the distress of refusing ; but when I heard of her loss, I felt that I positively could not stay away. I simply had to come—though my doctor looked grave, and my husband shook his head. 'You foolish people,' I said, 'you do not know the strength of a mother's feelings!' So here I am! I suppose there is *some* corner where Somers and I can be put for a couple of days ? I shall not be exacting for the very short time I can allow myself. Lord Mortlake insists upon my joining him the day after to-morrow. And I am the simplest creature, really! 'If my *maid's* comfort is attended to, I shall be all right,' I always say. It is the maid who is the really important person when one goes on a visit, and not the mistress. Oh, I assure you, if she is satisfied, that is everything!"

A little to Archie's surprise, Patricia seemed quite eager to see her mother.

"Did you send for her?"

"No; I did not think you were quite well enough yet for visitors."

"I am quite well. It won't hurt me." She flushed a faint red. "It is natural mamma should wish to see me."

"You shall see as much of her as you like," he said, with careful gentleness. "Only don't let her tire you. I'll tell nurse to tap at the door in half an hour; that will be enough for the first visit."

But Lady Mortlake was right in her estimate of herself; she was entirely out of her sphere in a sick-room. She rustled in with an elaborate caution that would have set even strong nerves on edge, and not a sentence that she uttered in her carefully-guarded undertone rang true. Her pose as the devoted, motherly mother would once have stirred Patricia's irreverent humour: it only struck her now with a chill sense of being forsaken.

"My darling child!"—a peck on Patricia's brow with careful lips, a caress of her thin hand, to which there was no response. "How sad to find you here! Oh, what I have suffered in thinking of you! They wanted to keep me away. They spoke of the long journey: they knew how easily everything affects me. But I insisted on coming. But, my own, you must not excite yourself—you must not, indeed, or your poor little mother will be turned out. Your Archie is a tyrant, as I told him; and that big, cross nurse will come and send her away." She spoke as if Patricia were about two years old.

"I am not excited, mamma." Patricia was gazing at her, seeing her with new, changed eyes. "I was her baby once," she thought. "Can motherhood do no more for poor women than this? If my child had lived, would she have turned from me, too, in the day of her sorrow? Why do I feel no thrill, no stir in me? I thought when Archie told me she was there I could cry on her breast; but she has on such a fine dress, tears would spoil it

—and—I haven't any tears. I think I am turned into a stone."

"Dear one, how you look at me with those big eyes!" said Lady Mortlake, playfully.

"You are very pretty, mamma—prettier than you used to be." It was odd, but Patricia felt as if she were acting in a play, saying words she had not rehearsed—that some one unseen prompted.

"I'm afraid I can't say the same of you, my child." The retort was given smilingly. "Such hollows here"—she laid soft finger-tips on Patricia's cheeks—"and such very solemn eyes. Do you always look so serious, darling? Of course," she added hastily, "you are thinking of the baby; but you mustn't, you really mustn't. It is a mercy the poor little pet was taken before it could suffer any more. That is how you must look at the thing, dear. That is the wise, sensible way."

"Yes, mamma," said Patricia with strange quiet, "I have learned my lesson quite perfectly already, and baby was only buried a week ago. It is a mercy she was taken, before she could suffer as women suffer."

Lady Mortlake looked a little disconcerted ; but she saved the situation by saying sentimentally—

"We do suffer," she spoke pensively ; "we poor women, we are all nerves, all emotions."

"You don't look very miserable," Patricia went on, in the same odd, quiet way. "You look as if you had got everything you expected to get when you married Lord Mortlake. That is all the happiness one can ask, isn't it ?"

"Dear child, what an odd way of putting it !" she spoke with soft reproach. "Of course, if I had not felt that my—my happiness and comfort would be safe in Lord Mortlake's care, I should never have married him. No one can say I was in a hurry to end my widowhood, and no one can tell how often I was tempted to do so—for your sake chiefly ; it is hard for a mother to deny her only child the luxuries and pleasures that are her birthright. You know how poor we were ; though your father had the title, everything else went from him. It was dreadfully hard—quite wicked, I think. You are a married woman yourself now, and you can understand what a struggle it was to keep up appearances on such a pittance."

"Yes, I think I can understand what marriage means ; but I don't think being poor would matter. There are so many worse things."

A faint expression of hardness began to show behind her ladyship's smiles, and her voice had an edge of annoyance.

"I was quite sure something was worrying you," she said; "you have so fallen off in looks, poor child. But I *do* hope, Patricia, you haven't been exceeding your income? This house is most expensively furnished "—she looked round her with a calculating eye; "you must have spent very nearly as much as we did in Eaton Place. We had Mortlake House to refurnish, too. I simply couldn't have lived with those dreadful, dreadful monstrosities the Dowager left behind her : they made me ill, so gloomy and ghostly, but it ended in our spending a mint of money. You have my refined tastes, and you know how expensive *real* art always is : but I must tell you at once, dear, you must not look to us to help you out of your difficulties. I really could not sanction any appeal to Lord Mortlake."

"Don't be alarmed, mamma. We pay all our bills quite punctually. The tradespeople will give us an excellent character, I believe, if you ask them."

"Then it must be your husband. Oh, my poor darling, I always had my fears that your marriage would turn out badly! I never really took to Dr. Sutherland, and I couldn't conceal from myself that he wasn't nearly good enough for you."

"Really ?" Patricia smiled faintly. "Yet you left us a great deal alone together. And you asked him frequently to dinner."

"A little absorption—a little selfishness even, might be excused in the circumstances ; " the retort was made with injured dignity. "When a woman contemplates a great change in her life, she is apt to be oblivious of the little concerns of others, at least if, as I hope I may say of myself, she is a serious-minded person. I have a very high standard, Patricia, a very exacting ideal, and I felt I must live up to it. If you accuse me of neglect, I must bear it; but that I should knowingly urge you to make an unhappy marriage!   Oh, that I should live to hear such a reproach!"

"Please don't run away with an idea," said Patricia, with flushed cheeks. "You are quite mistaken in thinking that Archie is unkind to me.   On the contrary, I have found him almost too kind, and I am sure that not even Lord Mortlake is so attentive and considerate as a husband."

"Then all I can say is that you should look happier, my dear, since you have nothing to complain of."

"I have certainly nothing to complain of." There was the light of kindled pride in her hazel eyes.

"It is a positive duty to look cheerful, however out of sorts you may feel," said this martyr in silk and costly lace; "and of course

I don't deny that we have a hundred thousand things to worry us our husbands never dream of."

"You don't look as if you worried much, mamma; you have no little lines or creases, and not a grey hair. Perhaps it is your standard that helps you? I think I must set up a standard too. I hadn't one when I became Archie's wife. I thought it would be all right if I cared for him enough."

"A wise woman," said Lady Mortlake, archly, "never lets her husband suspect that!"

"Why didn't you make me wise?" Patricia laughed a little odd laugh. "I was so very ignorant."

"She teaches him," Lady Mortlake went on, unheeding the interruption, "that she expects him to do all the caring. It keeps him in his proper place."

"But if he lived up to his standard he wouldn't require to be taught."

"Ah, now, when you argue, I begin to recognize my old Patricia! You were always so much cleverer than your poor little mother ; but really, dear, I thought you had grown positively dull ! Perhaps," she ended excusingly, " it is the Scotch climate or the Scotch surroundings that have affected you—so very sombre, so very, very serious ! "

" Perhaps," Patricia acquiesced. " It is certainly very difficult to be the right sort of Scotchwoman when you are not born to the business."

" But it is such a relief to me that you have not acquired the brogue ! That would have been a *real* affliction."

She said as much to Sutherland that evening when he came to the drawing-room for half an hour, as in duty bound.

" It is inexpressibly soothing to me to find my dear child happy and contented," she went on, after having expressed her pleasure in the unaltered refinement of Patricia's accent, as if its impairment were the chief calamity she had dreaded. " I was a little anxious ; why should I deny it ? So many matches turn out badly, and Patricia writes so seldom. After all, we knew very little about you, my dear Archie : not of course as to respectability, and all that "—she gave a little laugh ; "but that goes such a little way in marriage. There are the Castle people, for instance ; they say he beats her. and his pedigree is long enough. But. now that I have seen your home, and how nice and pretty it is, and have my dear Patricia's assurance that you make her the very best husband in the world, I shall go to my good man quite satisfied and comforted. The one thing I really couldn't brook would be to have my child coming back disappointed. I could never survive it !"

It is not so easy for a man as it is for a woman to dissemble suddenly stirred feelings. Poor Sutherland turned a deep, embarrassed red under this eulogium ; but if he feared scrutiny and detection, he might have spared himself the emotion. She saw what she chose to see, and believed that which it was comfortable and convenient to believe ; and having played out the little farce she had designed, would go away in much conceit of herself and her touching exhibition of devotion. Patricia did not ask her to prolong her visit, and accepted her excuses and regrets without remonstrance ; but when next Archie went to see her, she turned towards him for the first time voluntarily, and with a timid reviving of kindness in her glance.

"Mamma is gone ?"

"Yes ; Harry is escorting her to Edinburgh. It is a very short visit, but perhaps she will come back when you are better, and able to go about with her."

"Mamma and I have never gone about together since I was small enough to be dressed in Liberty smocks and look picturesque. I've outgrown sashes and pinafores ; I wouldn't set her off now. I think I am really a great deal older than she is."

"You will soon be well, and look as young as ever."

"Yes ; I think I might be moved to the sofa to-morrow, and soon I shall be able to go downstairs again. I think you and Mr. Fowler must want me to pour out the tea."

He did not dare to say that he had missed her; the miserable embarrassment of their estrangement tied his tongue; but he took the crumb of comfort gratefully, and when she said—

"You look very tired; you have been watching by me too long," he answered quite cheerfully—

"Oh, a little less sleep matters nothing to a doctor; the loss is easily made good since he can take it anywhere or anyhow, as well on horseback as on a feather bed."

CHAPTER X.

I WAS crossing the platform at Waverley Station after seeing our featherpate visitor safely on her way to meet her husband, when I came face to face with Frank Cunningham.

His greeting of me was more cordial than it might have been.

"How do you come to be here?" he asked. "I can't flatter myself that it was to meet me!"

"I knew you were expected, but hadn't heard when."

"I broke the journey at York. I was seedy with overwork and couldn't stand the right through business. But, first of all, tell me what's the latest news? How did you leave the poor old man?"

"I hadn't time to hear before starting this morning, but yesterday he was much the same. Sutherland is surprised, I think, that his strength holds out."

"It seems to me very sudden."

"You wouldn't say so if you had seen him within the last year."

He stopped a moment on the pavement; then he lifted his head with a movement I had learned to know, as if he would shake off some burdening reproach.

"It was no use. I couldn't come. But I'm glad I've managed it now."

There was some change in him I found it difficult to account for. He looked as if he had been taking some care of his health, his colour was clearer, his aspect younger, but he was restless and fell into fits of absentmindedness. Anxiety might have accounted for this, but it did not fit my conception of his character to imagine him much concerned about any one but himself. Perhaps I wronged him.

During the hour's journey he made himself quite a pleasant companion, chatting of the doings of that little London world of writing folk that always seems to those of us who are "landward bred," so much more important than it is. He spoke of Davidson lightly, with a touch of that patronage which a year or two earlier it had been Davidson's privilege to bestow. Davidson's last book had been a little too strongly flavoured even for the very accommodating digestion of the public, and for the instant he was somewhat under eclipse.

Of the brother and sister who had stood by Cunningham so gallantly in his need, he could tell me less than I already knew.

"I've left Mother Wembley's, you know," he said, "and in London you knock up against such a heap of people, you can never keep them all in mind."

Apparently he had allowed other and more important memories to be overlaid too, for, as we slowed on taking the curve before entering the station, he said, in a half bewildered, half amused way—

"By Jove, it's a sort of resurrection, coming back to the old place!"

That dangerous half-circle which the train describes as it crosses the Shaw is as if designed to group imposingly the crowding mills with their night splendour of windows ablaze with flashing lights ; and even above the thunder of the engine one can hear the throb of their ceaseless industry.

"Working night shifts," he said ; "that smacks of dull prosperity. I remember how, as a small boy, I used to steal off to the station at darkening, and look over there at Meikle and Todd's, and listen to the birr of the looms, and feel that I was somehow helping at the going round of the world! To be in the middle of that roar and rattle gave one a taste of doing. But what a snippet of life it is, after all! I'll wager you anything, in all those years between that time and now, there's not a single noddle here that has conceived a single idea beyond some trumpery trade improvement, possibly—and he has patented that, you may be sure—which is of any value to mankind."

"I suppose trade is of some small value." I said, nettled at his conceit; "we can't all shine in the literary world, but we must all wear clothes."

"True," he said, taking the retort quite good-humouredly; "but you needn't be a genius to manufacture tweeds."

"And is everybody a genius who chooses to dip his pen in ink?"

"Oh, there are dunces and dullards everywhere in a world that is more foolish than wise: but to rub shoulders with a few odd millions, most of them struggling to better you in the race, and nine out of ten depending on their wits to do it, gives a keener zest to the game of life. Those men who are the makers of Shawbridge were rich with inherited money when I went away—they are a little richer now. That's all their history. Money can't even do for them what it could do for you or me if we had it, for they don't know how to use it. It's the experience of Rip Van Winkle reversed to come here again; one has to travel back a hundred years to get on the old level.

Of course," he ended laughingly, realizing perhaps that as one of the sleepers I was scarcely in sympathy with this view. "there are people and places of which one wants to keep one's impressions unaltered by so much as a touch. Every man's home is a shrine. I'm speaking merely from the point of view of a Londoner—and with all his huge complacence — who finds himself condemned to temporary exile in the provinces."

"The provinces are mightily obliged to you for your condescension."

"Come and see me," he said, as we shook hands in the gusty station; "you're sneakingly in sympathy with me, though you won't own it. I saw you in my world, remember."

"Then, indeed, you saw a very disenchanted person!" I cried. "Your world, my good fellow, pleased me infinitely less than my own, which is no sham, at least."

He laughed.

"Then come for the sake of all you did for me," he said; "that's a reason you can't resist. Come, and overlook it if I can't return your visit. I shan't want to be much away from the Manse."

If only there had not been those little hints of feeling, that look, half mocking, half self-accusing in his dark eyes, it would have been easier to dislike him consistently.

But it was something to his account that he should have brought an expression of subdued happiness into Nancy's face, such as it wore when I went to the Manse. She was telling me how well the meeting between Frank and his father had gone off, when the minister came out of his study.

He greeted me with a curt nod; he looked irritable and heavy-eyed, as if he had slept badly.

Nancy passed a hand through his arm; the brightness faded out of her face as she looked at him; it became anxiously tender instead.

"Mr. Fowler has come to ask for the minister," she said. "Dear papa, Frank brought you a message that, if you could go to him this afternoon, his father would like to see you."

"My dear, do you think it necessary? Do you think it prudent?" said the minister, looking disturbed and embarrassed. "It seems to me that any agitation at such a time can only be harmful. I feel sure"—he looked at me, and I understood now that it was his hope I would back him—"I feel sure, Mr. Fowler, as—as a man of the world, will agree with me, that it would be kinder for the patient's sake to refuse."

"Since the suggestion comes from himself," I ventured; but Nancy turned upon him with pained reproach.

"Oh, papa, nothing can hurt him now—and —after all those years that we have lived next door and been friends—— Oh, you will not refuse to take him by the hand—for the last time."

"I trust, as a minister of the Gospel," Dr. Gillespie gathered pomposity as his courage revived, "I have always lived in peace and Christian charity, even with a brother whose courses I have been compelled to discountenance," he said, "but there has scarcely been that intimacy—that close connection between us that you would suggest by your talk of ' next door.' You give Mr. Fowler a wrong impression, Nancy. There has been no running out and in on *my* part, though I have been unable to control your actions. You have taken your own way," he said. with subdued bitterness, " in that as in other matters ; but naturally, in my position here, as the guardian of the Church's interests, as an example to my flock-——"

" Oh, where could they get a better example —a more saintly life to model their own by ? " said Nancy, with quick, hurt feeling. " And, papa, surely it is not the miserable, paltry differences on quite unimportant questions of Church discipline one should be thinking of now."

Whatever he might have said or done in other days, she was right when she cried out that he could not disobey this summons now. Perhaps he would have had no disinclination for that last farewell, have made no parade of those doctrinal points on which they held opposing views, had the Free Church minister been a little earlier in quitting this life. Half a dozen years before Dr. Gillespie was a proud man, holding his head high, ready to be kindly and graciously patronizing to a weaker neighbour; but now, though he still lifted his head as he walked about Shawbridge and received the greetings of his admiring people, it drooped before his daughter's anxious, loving gaze.

Poor minister: perhaps it was that guilty inner consciousness that to Nancy he was no hero, but a mere man, whom she must love still, indeed, but whom she must also support and guide, so that his feet should not stray in forbidden paths, that made him so bitter even while he yielded to her prayers. Tenderly as she sought to hide it even from herself, he was king in his own house no longer. From that day when he found her weeping the most hopeless tears a woman can weep, tears for another's shame and dishonour—he had manliness enough left to shudder away from the recollection—he knew himself discrowned, and

even the praise and applause of Shawbridge
was as dust and ashes in his mouth. But for
all that he was humiliated before himself and
abased, he could not forgive Nancy that she
knew. She knew, and her knowledge per
mitted her to do all things, gave her a licence
under which he winced, loving and doubly
dutiful and daughterly as she was. He had to
go when she put her arm within his and persuaded him to set out on that most unwilling
errand to the other Manse; he had to stand
aside even on his own hearth and see Frank
Cunningham made much of and welcomed,
Frank, whom he had held up as a warning
to his people in that famous sermon on the
Prodigal Son! What was he but a prodigal
himself, a long, long way strayed from
home? He made furtive search with hands
that trembled among his disordered papers for
that manuscript, eager to destroy it, and perhaps
efface the memory of it, not knowing that it
was already blown in ashes to the four winds
of heaven, and when Frank came knocking at
his door, and asking for Nancy, he had to come

out of his study and shake hands with him, wondering, with a new sting of anger, whether Frank had guessed or had been told anything—as if even Nancy might turn traitor to get her lover back unforbidden !

One or two of Mr. Cunningham's anxious, faithful people were waiting for news of him in the narrow lobby, and when Mr. Mackie, his chief elder, came out of the bedroom, he, like the rest, shook hands with Nancy as if she were one of themselves.

All this appropriation and appreciation of her was as gall and wormwood to her father, who, in the many years of his incumbency, had nicely balanced patronage and forbearance in his behaviour to these rebels gone over to the other camp, holding a certain dignity and distance necessary and becoming.   And now it was Nancy this and Nancy that—not even Miss Gillespie—as they crowded round her, talking and consulting, while he went alone into that inner room, once more converted into a sick-chamber.

But at sight of the pallid face turned

towards him in patient, smiling greeting, shame covered him, and he bowed his head; his eyes fell, as if those sightless ones could read the guilt and the fear in them.

"This is good of you," said the minister, in that faint, far-away voice, that seemed already to come from some great distance. "I felt sure you would come."

"I—I was glad to come," the other stammered, all his self-confidence gone from him. "If only to tell you how much we all hope you will still get quite well."

"Yes, yes," said the minister, for whom the words had but one meaning; "I shall soon be well. I have had a happy life—a full cup of blessings; and I have to thank you for making many things easy that might have been difficult."

"I"—faltered the visitor—"I—my dear friend—I have done nothing."

"You have done this, that you have lived in neighbourly peace and good-fellowship with me, when another might have made of our differences a cause of estrangement and bitterness. For that, my people have cause to be grateful to you, as their minister is; for you have set them an example of Christian forbearance I would fain hope they will not forget to follow when I am gone and another stands in my place. Extend your kindness to him, too, and I shall go without fear."

The minister took the hand that groped for his; but he had no words, not even to protest or cry out that he was undeserving of this praise. Even when there were broken whispers about Nancy—the daughter whom they shared—he had nothing to answer. He was overwhelmed.

"You will give her to Frank? He has not been worthy of her; but her love will make him deserving. Love must lift us all to our best."

He was dumb—his head bent on his breast, all that fine and gracious dignity, that so impressed Shawbridge, crushed out of him. In this thing, too, he must yield. Let Nancy take her way, marry the man whom he hated, but dared no longer despise, since but for love, patient, forgiving, shielding, to what deeps might not he, too, fall?

But he could not but go away out of that room, solemn with the shadow of death, softened, broken for the moment with emotion, vowing many changes in his heart. It gave him another pang when the minister said in his gentle way, and in that voice that was so weak and spent, and yet which carried such authority—

"We serve one and the same Master, and in His presence—where I shall soon be, and where you, too, will one day stand—we shall see, eye to eye, our differences forgotten. But it is good, for the cause of Christ, which we both serve, that you, in your place of trust, have been able to rise above them here. You will let a dying man pray that He will continue to bless and prosper you in your work?"

How could he but go out overwhelmed, ashamed, knowing in his heart how far he had been from fulfilling that high ideal, and yet not without a little comfort too. A vain man, and weak, it restored a little of his tarnished self-respect that another, to whose blameless life all men bore witness, believed in him, thought the best of him. He had almost hated Nancy for finding him out; but he did not hate the minister, whose simple, cordial words of kindness were as balm to his inward irritation.

He slipped out of the glass door, left a little ajar for air, and stole unseen by the garden and field path to his own house, locking himself in his study there. It was the most searching hour of his life, this first glimpse of himself in all the nakedness of unclothed shame, not draped any more, or decorated with sham virtues; but a man who had dared to rebuke the sin in others which he practised and cherished in himself. The ensample to his flock, and himself a castaway.

For Frank, too, whatever he may have suffered on his account—and he knew more, perhaps, than we others, unless it were Sutherland—guessed, the old man had only words of a fine cheer, and hope, and blessing, behind which his own sorrow was never allowed to peep. And Frank was touched—all his better emotions brought to the front, his quick, delicate, half-feminine ways under service. Even Sutherland was forced to own that the young fellow, who had made so poor a patient, was unrivalled as a nurse. Not Nancy herself could turn a pillow or support the invalid and lift him into an easier position with greater tact and deftness. Everybody yielded place to him, rather grudgingly, perhaps, recognizing his right, though he had been so long in claiming it, to the seat by the pillow, the watch through the long, black hours; and the minister's face reflected the peace that lay upon his spirit, at rest from all vexation.

Perhaps Frank did not recognize the fine magnanimity, the large charity of the older man; but his emotional nature found a certain artistic satisfaction in the scene, and in his own tender and wholly dutiful part in it. In the broken talks between the long silences, he first heard the story of his own life.

"Your mother was the only woman I ever loved," the minister said : "but she had given her heart elsewhere—and she only knew me as a friend who would not fail her. She left you as a legacy to me—a very precious trust—when she died."

Frank's vanity was piqued. He had so long imagined a quite different setting to his early story, and had been pleased, in a melancholy way, to think that it was his own childish beauty and charm—seen against a background of cruel parents, come down mysteriously from some high place in the world by reason of vices that were half picturesque, since they were the failings of high-born folk—that had touched and moved the minister to compassion. It was romantic as a schoolgirl's dream, silly and absurd, yet, though he had humour enough to laugh at it, his vanity was ruffled too. It had given a certain sanction to his weakness to imagine himself the victim of inherited tendencies, against which it was useless to struggle ; and behold, there was no mystery wrapping and clouding his birth at all. His mother had been a pretty girl, a little lower in social status than the minister whose love she was, and distinguished only by a certain simple goodness, and the man she had married had been equally respectable and equally unremarkable. In his nettled annoyance he did not think of the pathetic light in which this unrequited and unspoken affection placed the minister, and indeed of himself in that aspect the minister thought not at all.

"I took you to my heart and my home for your mother's sake," he said; "but in a very little while I forgot that you had not always been my own."

And Frank had the grace to tell himself that here was a history, better than the bravest he could have composed for himself—to be the child of so loyal and noble a love as this ; and perhaps he wished, as we so vainly do when the chance to make good our offences has gone by, that he had not wounded and repulsed it so often.

So, very gently and quietly, with the two he loved best beside him, and many others sorrowing and sympathizing near, he faded into the last sleep, out of which he did not wake. The spring night was clear, after a day of sharp searching wind, and the sky was thick sown with stars. They described the face of heaven to him—it was his nightly request.

"Be eyes for me, and tell me of the sky."

Once or twice, wandering a little, perhaps, in his weakness, he murmured of "the patines of bright gold," shining through heaven's floor, and once, clearly and almost gaily, of "the country beyond Orion;" and in the morning when they bent over him to wake him he had travelled thither.

All the minister's little property, with the exception of an annuity for his old servant, had been left to Frank without reserve, it being understood, of course, that Nancy would share it; but though it would make, when realized, a welcome addition to his small revenues, the business connected with it was irksome to him, and provoked some little display of unamiability in others. Though it had been universally acknowledged that he had behaved very well in the sick-room, Cunningham knew himself no favourite with his father's flock. It was remembered how seldom he had troubled himself to come back to the home that had sheltered him, and vague, half-forgotten stories touching his birth were circulated once more to prove that nothing very good could be expected of him. During the greater part of the ten days which were all he could spare after the funeral, melancholy preparations for dismantling the little home were going on. The thought that the familiar furniture, shabby and valueless as it was, was to be sold, went to Nancy's heart. Yet all the arguments Cunningham used were quite reasonable and sensible. He pointed out that the furniture was old-fashioned, and yet not old enough to have any money value.

"It would take a little fortune to cart it to town," he said, "and even if we got it there for nothing, it could never be squeezed into a modern flat, and leave us room to turn round. You're forgetting in what a modest way we'll have to set up, Nancy."

What cared she how modest it was—a little house, a fifth floor flat—a but and ben, even, so long as they were together; but for all that, her heart yearned over what he called "the old sticks."

"Perhaps, by the time we are married, you will be able to take a larger house," she said.

"Not very likely, between now and summer!" he retorted, with a laugh. "Do you suppose, now that I am able to keep you, though it won't be in any sort of grand way, I am going to wait any longer?"

This was another trouble to Nancy, those allusions he was always making to their immediate marriage. A little while ago, how her heart would have leaped at the thought; but now—— She dashed aside the tears that would rise for her own disappointment; she would not tell him now—while he had so much to fret and worry him—that they could not be married this summer, perhaps not the following summer either. That vision of the little home somewhere in the vast heart of London, where they were to begin an ideal life together, so long encouraged, so near realization, must be put away for yet a while longer. By-and-by, some day, it would all come true—she still fed her fainting heart on that hope—some day she would be free, as she was not free now.

The hardest thing of all was to explain this to Frank, who had so long seemed careless if not reluctant, and who was now almost fretfully eager that everything should be settled before his return to town.

"What is there to wait for?" he demanded, when Nancy, faint-hearted at the task before her, hinted at delay. "Haven't we been long enough engaged, in all conscience? We've let all the boys and girls who were mere babies when we fell in love with each other outstrip us. They are old, sober married folks, while we're still dangling on as lovers."

"Is it so bad to be lovers, Frank?"

"The general judgment is against long engagements," he said, with a laugh, "and the general judgment is generally right. We haven't quarrelled yet, Nancy; but we're human, and who knows, if we delay much longer we may grow tired of each other, and fall out."

"Don't say that, Frank, even in fun."

"Well, my dear, make it impossible by promising in earnest that you'll be my wife before the summer is over."

"Before summer," she echoed, scarcely knowing what she said, with the thick beating of her heart in her ears. Her eyes were large with a frightened, piteous appeal. "Oh, not quite so soon!" she pleaded. "You will be patient—we have both been patient—we have waited so long, it won't be so very hard to wait a little longer. It may not be so very long, but not this summer."

"And why not this summer?" he questioned, a little annoyed and perplexed, but not losing patience still. "Nancy, you haven't—surely you can't possibly imagine it would be disrespectful to the—to my father's memory? I know women have odd notions about mourning."

"It isn't that," she said eagerly, glad to

speak freely. "How could it be, when you know he would have liked to marry us himself—if—if there had been time."

"Well, if it isn't that—and of course he expected and hoped we should not delay—what is it?"

"Oh, there are so many things! How can I explain?" she said distractedly. "There is my father to be considered, Frank."

His face darkened.

"I thought we had agreed that we had a right to settle our own lives," he began; but she laid an imploring hand upon his sleeve.

"Be patient with me, dear. I am yours, all yours, as much as ever; and papa will not object."

"He has always objected," he said, with a hard laugh. "I can't pretend that he ever cared for me, and it is plain enough he doesn't relish the thought of me as a son-in-law; but he has given his consent, and it's a little late in the day, isn't it, to begin to have scruples? If you have changed your mind——"

"You hurt me, dear, when you speak like

that. How could I change? There has never been any one but you, there never will be any one else. I should have to be made over again if I could change. And papa has said nothing. But I must think of him a little too, as well as of my own happiness." In her agitation, she spoke almost incoherently. How could she make him agree to her wishes without explaining, and to explain was so wholly impossible; at the bare thought of such an infidelity, the blood burned in her face. "I am all he has," she faltered; "it will be so lonely for him. We must give him time to grow accustomed to the thought."

"I should have thought he had had a good deal of time," he said coldly. "You can scarcely pretend that he will be taken by surprise."

"But so soon! Summer is almost here; and he would be quite alone! We have no relations, or none who could come to be with him, and to leave him with Ann—with only a servant—good as Ann is——"

"Don't you think you're exaggerating

matters?" he said, making a great effort to speak with moderation. "I'm not going to say he won't miss you, for of course he will; but he will miss you less than many a man would who was more domestic, who had fewer friends and outside interests. Look how he goes about; he's scarcely ever at home. He has the social instinct; he has the knack of being popular. You needn't worry, Nancy; if he misses you at first, he'll soon learn to get along without you. He has only to show himself willing to go in, and a dozen doors will fly open to him. So, if that's your only reason, it's no reason at all."

He had said nothing that was harder than this to bear, because it was all true. Her father would not miss her, would perhaps even find it a relief that she was gone, and that there was only Ann, who was a servant without authority, without the right to check or even to guard him, left at home. She had not misread that look of furtive annoyance on his face, of something that might any day break out into open resentment and rebellion, when she steadily accepted the invitations that came for herself as well as for him, and dressed in her hateful finery, and ate the dinners that almost choked her. She was not always wanted at those dinners where her father's company was so highly prized, either by the hosts to whom she was only an extra woman to be provided with a partner, where there were already so many women, or by the minister, who was not quite so genial or natural, so condescending or gracious when she was by, conscious perhaps of the fears she could not wholly hide. It made him angry and restless to think that she was watching him with those sorrowful eyes; and she knew it, and her heart bled with the pain of it.

"It is my duty to stay with him a little longer," she said at last, speaking brokenly. "Bear with me, Frank; give me my own way in this one thing. Do not ask me to leave him this summer. He has not been so well and strong as usual. You said yourself you thought him changed—grown older. He is not young; and people who are past middle life like to have time to grow used to things. It would make me unhappy if I thought I had neglected him. Dear, you would not like me to take my joy at the expense of duty?"

"You've a queer notion of duty," he said, keenly offended. "Do you think you owe none to me? Haven't I worked and slaved"—perhaps, for the moment, he really believed in his own unshaken earnestness of purpose—"to get a little home together; and when, for the first time for all those years, I'm in a position to offer you the sort of surroundings you've been used to, you turn upon me, and tell me you can't leave your father! You are behaving very badly—you are trifling with me, Nancy! You have led me on all these years, and now, at the very end, you've grown tired of it all. You want to get out of it. And you talk of your father as if he were decrepit or imbecile, and you must watch him—your father, who is perfectly well able to take care of himself, and amuse himself, too, without you! I have not deserved this."

"I know, I know!" she said, her hands held out in entreaty, her face all quivering with pain and distress. "Forgive me, Frank—oh, forgive me!"

"Forgive you—for casting me off without any reason?"

"No, no; not casting you off! How can you dream of that? Only asking you to wait a little. Dear, be reasonable! Is it so very hard to grant me a month or two to—to set things in order at home? I have made no preparations, and there are many things to arrange. The summer will soon go by, and after that it might be easier—one might see one's way more clearly."

"Have you waited till now to see your way?" he asked, not unnaturally incensed and mortified. "I think you owe me some explanation, Nancy. You are blowing hot and cold—you are keeping something back. If you are tired of it all—if you think you've made a mistake, it would be honester to say so."

"How could I have made a mistake?" she said, almost despairing of convincing him, and feeling wretchedly how badly she was playing her part. "As for an explanation—there is nothing to explain."

"If there is some one else——" he said, and stopped short.

"It is cruel of you to say that!" she cried, indignant in her turn, and not deigning to rebut the accusation. "You only say it to hurt me!" But she was secretly a little glad that his mind should go away on these new lines, even if he were for the moment to pretend that she could be false and faithless.

It was not, perhaps, very difficult to convince him that he had no cause to be jealous, but for the rest he was not so easily appeased. He was fighting, though she did not know it, against his own baser instincts.

He had really struggled to work steadily, so as to lay by enough for the beginnings of their modest housekeeping, when it would have been so much easier to let things drift.

His marriage with Nancy was a sign to himself that he was to outstep the follies and frailties of the past and begin anew. With her to work for, everything would be different; not always so pleasant or so care-free, perhaps, but his life would have a purpose, his work a motive. It would be possible to achieve great things. But if she no longer cared—he was confounded, offended, inclined, in his irritation, to shake himself free; to show her that he could live his own life—the easier, jollier life—very well without her.

And if poor Nancy had known, what could she have done but weep still more bitter tears in secret?

It was hard when, melting again, and ashamed of his roughness, he began to pour into her ear all the plans he had made, the houses he had looked over—the one which he would take if she approved. The allurement of it all nearly carried her away. The little house which they were to make cosy together, the fun of furnishing—she had had so little fun in her life—of choosing pretty things for this nest, and contriving and planning together, so that it should be more charming than any other house, and yet without extravagance. And then the wonder of London, with its heady, exhilarating taste—London, where she had never set foot; but where people read and thought, and looked upon art and listened to music, and cultivated and polished their souls and minds—to live with Frank there, and see him take his share, and to meet and, perhaps, to talk with the clever men and women he knew—who could, even the least of them, teach her so much—all this passed as in a vision before her, and tempted her—oh, so hotly!—to yield. Just to take this beautiful existence that was offered her, that was hers by right, and to leave everything else, her troubles and fears and that sad, self-imposed guardianship, behind.

"Frank needs me." Always, since she could choose for herself, she had shaped her life to that thought. She was there to stand by him, to help him in all the ways that a woman could help a man; and now that he was waiting—calling to her, claiming her, she must turn aside and refuse to listen.

It was the saddest, most overwhelming moment she had had to face, because behind her courage, and the hope she would not let slip, lay the sickening fear that in sending Frank away now she was losing him altogether.

Neither of them, of course, hinted at such a thing, and they patched up a peace, with a shocked feeling in both hearts that to quarrel there—in the little garden where the minister's slow step, and the thud of his stick, still seemed to sound upon the gravel path—was a thing not to be thought of for a moment.

But though Frank yielded with a good grace in the end, and they talked vaguely of "by-and-by," instead of counting the summer days so quickly approaching, he went back to London with a sore feeling that somehow he had not had his dues. He had made a great effort, and Nancy had treated it lightly. He was accustomed to praise from her, and surrender and submission, and he took it ill that she stood out against him now. Surely she was a little unreasonable, a little capricious. He nursed the grievance as he went back in the train, though he kissed and forgave her when they parted under the rowan tree at the gate.

And she, poor soul, said to herself, watching him, "if he turns at the corner and waves to me, it will be a good omen;" but he, wrapped in his own thoughts, went on unheeding.

CHAPTER XI.

THE spring melted into summer.   Patricia made a good recovery; but, so far as I could see, Sutherland and she drew no nearer to each other.   Perhaps I missed the signs a woman was quicker to read, for when I confided my gloomy fears to Nancy, she only smiled.

"Oh, you men, you men, how blind you are! Where are your eyes?" she asked.

I protested that they were useful enough for all ordinary purposes, but that they could not see through a stone wall; and it seemed to me that nearly as impenetrable a barrier had risen between husband and wife.

"I advise you to get spectacles," she said,

and would not be coaxed or threatened into any kind of explanation.

With June a spell of hot weather set in, and Sutherland suddenly decided that Patricia, who looked pale and languid, must go to the sea.

"Why can't we all go together?" I asked. "A little roughing of it won't hurt any of us. Patricia keeps us too sleek and pampered."

At my suggestion the colour leapt into her face, and she threw me a glance of approval.

"Let's all go and be uncomfortable in lodgings," I went on, emboldened, but wondering what was signified by that brightening of her eyes. "You want a holiday more than any of us, Sutherland. I don't know if you know it, but you're getting to look quite ten years more than your age."

"All the better for my practice," he said carelessly. "A venerable aspect is a fortune to a doctor. I'm afraid I can't go; but perhaps"—he turned to his wife—"Miss Gillespie might arrange to join you, and Harry could look you up now and then."

"Very well, I will ask her," said Patricia, gentle and acquiescent as usual. She made no protest about being sent away alone, and when Sutherland spoke vaguely of possibly managing to get away for a week end, she only said, in her usual even tones, that she hoped he would. But when he had left the room she turned upon me.

"Do you really think he looks—older?" she demanded.

"He's over thirty. You can't expect him to keep looking like a boy, and the worries of a Shawbridge practice would age anybody."

"I thought he was getting on so well," she said, occupying herself with the bit of stuff she was sewing. "I heard some one say at the Plummers' the other day that he had carried everything before him."

"As far as work goes—but that only doubles the anxiety; and I'm afraid there's more honour and glory than money in the business."

"The honour and glory are best," she said a little proudly, not ill-pleased, I think, to hear him praised, since she could remember and repeat what a stranger had said of him.

My hint about money passed her by unnoticed, and perhaps it was only my fancy that we were living in too lavish a way. Sutherland never inquired how she spent her revenues, and probably had no idea how largely they went to supplement the housekeeping allowance he made her. Both he and she were naturally freehanded, and she had accustomed us to a certain fastidious daintiness that was more costly than it appeared to be. The ordering of her house occupied her a great deal at this time, she was always adding something to it to make it still more perfect; but even if Sutherland realized that their expenditure was out of proportion to their income, he would have been very slow to thwart her in anything that could give her pleasure. He owed it to her, at least, to see that her tastes and whims were gratified.

It chanced that Nancy could not arrange to leave home, and a day or two later Patricia told us at breakfast that she had had a letter

from Mrs. Tom Carnegie, inviting her on a
visit. Mrs. Tom had now a little home of her
own at Richmond; and, since the colonel was
taking a run abroad and would not be of the
party, Sutherland readily assented to Patricia's
suggestion that Richmond might be as pleasant
as a sojourn at the sea.

He saw her off a few days later, insisting
that she should take one of the maids with
her, and careful to the minutest detail for
her comfort. It was the first journey she had
gone upon since their brief honeymoon, and
now she was setting out alone. What were
they both thinking of, I wondered, as I said
good-bye to her on the doorstep, and what
was to come of it all?

I did not see Sutherland till evening, when
he managed to get home in time for dinner.
As we sat down to the meal she had been so
careful to arrange for us, we both missed her,
I think. Sutherland looked across the flowers
and the little silver bon-bon dishes to her
empty place, and said, with an attempt at
lightness, that here were we, two deserted

bachelors, left to our own devices once more.

But the bachelor days would not come back at a word. I had hoped, meanly perhaps, that, if we must lose Patricia—and if he missed her, did not I, who was her daily comrade?—at least I should have him to myself as in the long past. We should talk of everything under heaven and on earth, smoke as many pipes as we pleased, drink whisky and water, and sit on into the small hours with nobody to make us afraid. But these things were not to be. Sutherland was harassed with work—he had neither the time nor perhaps the inclination for the old outpourings, or even the old wordless silences when it was enough for us to be together. He was restless, a trifle captious, and even if he were not called out, would soon take himself off to his surgery, where I seldom followed him.

Patricia wrote to him twice or thrice a week, but beyond telling me that she was well and enjoying herself, he never spoke of her. Often he was the first to go down to breakfast, and

had already read and pocketed her letter before
I came in. I know that he answered her
punctually, for I saw the envelopes addressed
in his clear firm hand lying on the hall table
for the boy to post. Whether these things
were signs Nancy expected me to decipher I
cannot tell, I only realized mournfully that
we were as Jonathan and David no more.
What he had in his mind I was no longer
permitted to share.

At the conclusion of her visit to Mrs. Tom,
Patricia wrote that Mortlake and her mother
were going to Norway for the summer, and
were urgent that she should join them.
Sutherland had learnt to school his face
pretty well, but it was plain to see he was
disappointed, though he said, of course she
must go, and it was a capital chance for her
to get the change of air she needed.

He would take no holiday himself, though
I urged him to go to her if it were only for a
week, and, as if to make this impossible, when
Black broke down and was forced to rest,
Archie took over his work as well as his own.

About this time the question of the drainage of Hill Street cropped up again, and Sutherland must needs plunge himself into the very heart of the controversy; it was a storm in a tea-cup, but it roused a good deal of local ill-feeling, and Sutherland's popularity received a decided check. It was true he could hit pretty hard, and his letters to the Shawbridge *Pioneer* were certainly not models of meekness. Provost and Town Council were ranged against him. The faction that assembled under Mrs. Laidlaw's flag had no good word for him; something of the old antagonism that had embittered our first years in Shawbridge was stirred, and people began to ask each other whether, after all, he was so wonderfully clever? A doctor's reputation is a ticklish thing, blown upon by every wind, and he took no pains to conciliate public opinion. To one who looked on, it seemed as if he rather welcomed strife and controversy, and found some relief for pent-up feelings in the hard blows he dealt.

Patricia sometimes wrote to me while she

was upon her travels. Her letters were charming; they had a new note in them, betraying greater mental maturity; they showed her to be keenly observant, with an eye for the unusual and the humorous; they were full of sparkle and lightness. If she wrote in this strain to her husband, why did he frown and look moody each time he received a letter from her? Didn't he profess himself in the same breath to be immensely glad that she was recovering her health and spirits?

"She ought to come home," I ventured once; "it's three months since she left us."

"You haven't been telling her that?" he questioned sharply.

"No; I leave you to do that."

"She mustn't be hurried," he said; "she must fix her own time. She's evidently enjoying herself."

I suppose I was a fool not to understand. Her letters to him were no doubt quite as delightful as those she penned to me. They were frank, pleasant, amusing; but he was waiting for something, some sign or token he never found there. So pride was roused, and he would not recall her.

Thus month after month slipped by, and on one pretext or another Patricia still lingered. She had met some old friends in Norway, and had promised to visit them on her return to town. She had shopping to do; a fresh excuse was ever forthcoming for delay. She always asked Sutherland's permission very prettily, and, needless to say, at once obtained it; but such pleasure as was going all fell to her share—it was dull enough with us.

It was early winter before she came home, and my very first glance at her face told me it was a different Patricia who had returned. She looked the picture of blooming health and beauty. Her figure had rounded out and lost its angularity, her face its girlish thinness, her expression was self-reliant and serene. In a word, she had left us a child and come back a woman, self-controlled, with a delightful dignity, gracious, charming.

Sutherland could not take his eyes off her, but she appeared not to notice his

half-embarrassed wonder. She met his eyes
with a smile in her own which seemed to say,
" Do not be afraid of me, I will never trouble
you with my foolishness again."

She bore herself towards him with easy
frankness, as a sister might to a brother;
her talk no longer betrayed effort or con-
straint. She chatted spontaneously, was lively
on the subject of her travels, rallied us over
our relapse into untidiness, declared it would
take her months to bring us back to the level
of civilization at which she had left us.

Here we seemed to pick up the old Patricia,
but the next moment we lost her again. She
no longer railed at the practice after her old
manner, or hung about her husband delaying
his outset, teasing him to know when he
would come back to her, watching for him
at the appointed hour. She neither shrank
from him nor seemed to court his presence.
She had always a pleasant welcome for him
when she chanced to be at home at the hour
of his return; but she had taken up her social
duties with a great deal of vigour, and had

many affairs of her own to engross her. When he found me sole occupant of drawing-room, or dining-room, it seemed to me his step lost something of its spring, his brow clouded.

"Patricia out again?" he would say. "Does it take every day of the week to return calls in Shawbridge?"

Once, almost diffidently, for it was he who was ill at ease now, he said something to this effect to her.

"Have I really been out so much?" she said carelessly.

"I haven't found you at home since Saturday."

"Then I must amend my ways," she said, with light good-humour. "Has Harry been converting you to the delights of afternoon tea?"

What ailed the man that he should be discontented? A year ago he would have welcomed this sweet reasonableness; he had had to exercise patience then, her girlish ardour wearied him, her demonstrative affection sometimes bored him. She was very little likely to trouble him with any exhibition of tenderness now; and yet he was not satisfied. Her frank comradeship left him hungering; it almost repulsed him, and yet he could not keep away from her. He took to coming home at odd times; if he did not neglect his work, he no longer made it an excuse to absent himself. In the evenings, when Patricia was absorbed in a book, or bent over her needle-work, he would watch her behind his newspaper. Her profile was very pretty, she had a new way of doing her hair; her dress was either new or she wore it with more distinction. Was he making the discovery that he had married a very attractive woman?

She sat with calm stillness as if quite unconscious of, or indifferent to his scrutiny. Was she really indifferent? Once or twice I had seen the colour flutter into her cheeks at the unexpected sound of his latchkey; but when she looked up at his entrance, I could have sworn I was mistaken, for her face expressed nothing at all but readiness to be agreeable, to talk or be silent according to his desire.

She threw herself with a great deal of vivacity into the Hill Street controversy. I found her one day with a pile of old *Pioneers* she had rescued from the shelves of the store cupboard. The grubby sheets, ringed here and there with the mark of jam pots, contained the letters with which Sutherland had endeavoured to demolish his opponents.

"I am trying to understand the question," she explained, colouring a little, but speaking with dignity. "One must hear both sides."

"You hear the other side when you make your calls, I suppose?"

"Why didn't you send me these?" she asked, evading the question.

"What? You didn't want to mix up our muddy little politics with the splendours of Norway?"

"We must give some dinners," she said, as if determined I should have no direct reply. "Everybody asked us; it is time we paid our debts."

She broached the subject that evening. Sutherland acquiesced, as he must needs have acquiesced in any wish of hers, and the invitations were forthwith sent out, and most of them were promptly accepted—curiosity overcoming scruple. Patricia's disarming, all-conquering airs had left their impression. She took the greatest possible trouble with her table. On the evening of the first dinner, Sutherland, as he went upstairs to dress, caught a glimpse of her through the open dining-room door, and, turning, went in. He was in a mood of dull depression, hating Shawbridge, and despising the guests he was about to entertain. For a moment he stood looking at Patricia unobserved. She was absorbed in studying the general effect of her arrangements, her head a little on one side. When she saw him she smiled.

"Do you think it pretty?" she said. "I noticed that colour scheme in purple and blue in a flower-shop in town. I was afraid it might be a little bold; but it goes with the Venetian glass, doesn't it?"

"It is perfect," he said; but he was looking at her. It was a long time since he had seen her in full evening dress. She had never before looked so distinguished; but, alas, never so far off.

A flower she had worn in her bosom dropped. He stooped hurriedly to pick it up, and, in rising, his arm brushed against her almost with the effect of a caress. He coloured deeply, and for a moment her cheeks had an answering flush; but she only said lightly—

"Oh, thanks; how badly I must have secured it!"

The dinners and the dance she later gave for the younger folk had quite a little reputation. Patricia surpassed herself as hostess, and, though it was not to be expected she could all at once convert dour, bailie bodies to the merits of the newest sanitation, she certainly did something to restore confidence in her husband. For that season, at least, there was no such popular person in Shawbridge as young Mrs. Sutherland.

But her reign was destined to be very brief. Fate, the mistress of events, was preparing even then to meddle with our lives.

One afternoon in early summer I saw Sutherland come slowly across South Place; his walk was spiritless, his head bent, his whole air woke in me a vague alarm, and when he let himself in with his latch-key, and, contrary to his usual custom, went straight to his room, I determined to follow him.

Patricia was at the piano in the drawing-room. She had lately taken to diligent practice.

As I opened the door, he looked up from the writing-table, where he had seated himself, with a face of grey and haggard trouble.

"What is it?" I cried, my heart giving sick thumps.

In a very few words he told me. The company in which the too sanguine Mortlake had invested Patricia's money had failed, and her entire income was clean swept away beyond hope of recovery.

"Is that all?" I asked, thinking in the first moment of relief, that it was not so very terrible after all.

"All!" he cried fiercely. "My God! Isn't it enough that I married her only to make her hate me, and now I must drag her down to my own poverty? I got the letter this morning before I went out; but I couldn't face her. I don't know how I'm going to tell her now. I've been looking into things. We've been spending without a thought. There are debts. I couldn't stop on here unless we moved into a much smaller house." He gave a miserable laugh. "Think of Patricia in a forty-pound house with a maid-of-all-work! She'd better go back to her mother, if she'll have her. That fool, Mortlake, has lost a lot himself in this d——d company. If she cared for me I shouldn't mind two straws. I could work for her, but"—his head dropped again—"poor child, poor child, I've managed to kill her affection. That's the bitterness of it, Harry; there's nothing to make it easy for her."

Was there not? And if she were not hopelessly alienated, would not this common trouble soften her? At least, there was a chance.

I slipped from the room — he scarcely noticed my going—and went to her. She stopped her music at the sight of me—her hands resting on the keys. She listened admirably. She never moved nor spoke while I told my tale ; but when I said to her—

"He's wretched, Patricia ; because, he says, he has made you hate him," the colour came back with a rush to her white cheeks, the light to her eyes.

"Hate him ? " she said, in a low voice.

Oh, the dull, blind fool I had been !

"Come," I said. She rose, and hand in hand we went to the study.

The sound of the opening door roused him from the apathy into which he had fallen. He glanced up listlessly, but at sight of her his face changed and worked—amazement, dread, hope, all were there. He got up, his great frame shaking. He took a step forward stumblingly. He held out his hands, but let them fall again.

"Patricia ! " he said hoarsely.

I heard her give a little tremulous laugh,

that was half a sob. She did not wait for him to come to her. Both of them had forgotten me, and better so. I shut the door softly, and went away.

*   *   *   *   *

There is very little more to tell.

The practice in Shawbridge was sold, and Sutherland and Patricia settled in London. For several years they had something of a struggle to make ends meet; but they faced their difficulties cheerfully, and have long since surmounted them. Sutherland's brain was a capital that did not take wings. His book on "Diseases of the Joints" brought him into prominence, and he is now in a fair way to make himself a name. Lady Mortlake has ceased to regard his residence in London as a personal offence, and will probably be satisfied that Patricia has not done so very badly when Sutherland is made a baronet, and has moved to Cavendish Square; and if he is permitted at the same time to take account of the pulse of royalty, she will persuade herself that she has always foreseen his success, and laboured to forward it. Even now she likes to take the elder children—who are very pretty, and always charmingly dressed—out with her for an airing in the carriage, and is never more delighted than when people tell her it is quite utterly impossible that she can be a grandmother.

No one was very much surprised when, two years after her husband's death, Cunningham married Sophia Blythe.

It was said by some that Nancy broke off her engagement at her father's pleading; others, who knew Cunningham, said that he had grown weary of waiting, and had not been able to stand the test of a long engagement. The affair made a great stir in Shawbridge. Mrs. Laidlaw was jubilant; but Nancy's best friends felt that she had had a lucky escape. What she herself felt remained unrevealed. One was left to infer, from one's knowledge of her character, what a wrench her whole nature must have received—all that had been her life, her hope, her consolation, come to nothing. It was a year after Cunningham's marriage before we again met, and though she looked older and graver, her face had recovered its serenity. It brightened into real happiness when she told me that her father had been elected Moderator of the General Assembly—a picturesque and dignified office he was well fitted to adorn. Her manifest and legitimate pride in him was all the reward her heart desired for the sacrifice of her life to his.

Patricia still clings fondly to the belief that Nancy will some day find a worthier mate, and marry and live happily ever after.

She may be right; but, for my part, I do not think Nancy is the person to love twice.

It would be absurd to paint Cunningham as a man devoured by remorse, or even at all unhappy. His marriage is supposed to be quite successful, and he would himself say that he and his wife jog along capitally together. It is his instinct to be kind when everything goes well with him; he likes to sun himself in his prosperity, and never forgets that he owes it to Sophia; while she prizes his crumbs of kindness more than the plentiful meal her worthier first husband would have spread before her. And as it is only old-fashioned and romantic people who expect more than this of marriage, they may be pronounced quite an exceptionally fortunate couple.

True he has written no more books, and this is a little disappointment Sophia has to swallow in silence. She had pictured herself as the wife of a distinguished man, praised of the people; but she took away the spur when she shared with him her new-gotten wealth. Regarding Nancy, one can only make a guess at their feelings, but it is probable they constructed a comfortable theory that she had behaved badly, and that in snatching at their own happiness, they were not depriving her of anything she deserved to possess.

Young Flower passed his final triumphantly, and is looking forward to making before long a home which his sister can share with him.

When last we heard from Shawbridge, Mrs. Laidlaw was still alive, very old and infirm, but with undiminished interest in the concerns of others. Her wings, however, are clipped, and she is no longer a power in the land.

A new generation has sprung up, made of bolder stuff than were the Nancies and Patricias of an earlier day, a generation that scorns the intermeddling of age, that makes its own laws and settles its own fate.

Doubtless these cheerful and confident young spirits who fall out and come together again, and love and marry without the slightest regard for their elders—who are indeed conveniently disposed of on their appointed shelves—would stare with the honestest wonder if it were whispered to them in what fear and trembling we went of Shawbridge's mischief-maker.

"What! Afraid of that old thing?" they would cry, with undisguised scorn. "A mere bundle of bones dragged about in a Bath-chair. She couldn't frighten a fly!"

Looked back upon here in careless London, and from the safe distance of years, her despotism does seem rather absurd. But, however apologetic one may feel, the fact remains.

She did her best to wreck more than one young life, and it is no thanks to her that she did not succeed.

THE END.

PRINTED BY WILLIAM CLOWES AND SONS, LIMITED,
LONDON AND BECCLES.   G., C. & Co.

www.ingramcontent.com/pod-product-compliance
Lightning Source LLC
Chambersburg PA
CBHW020937120726
47905CB00008B/2556